A Package at Gitmo

Jerome Brown and His Military Tour at Guantanamo Bay, Cuba

A novel

PAUL BOUCHARD

iUniverse, Inc.
Bloomington

A Package at Gitmo
Jerome Brown and His Military Tour at Guantanamo Bay, Cuba

iUniverse books may be ordered through booksellers or by contacting:

iUniverse
1663 Liberty Drive
Bloomington, IN 47403
www.iuniverse.com
1-800-Authors (1-800-288-4677)

Because of the dynamic nature of the Internet, any Web addresses or links contained in this book may have changed since publication and may no longer be valid. The views expressed in this work are solely those of the author and do not necessarily reflect the views of the publisher, and the publisher hereby disclaims any responsibility for them.

The views expressed in Paul Bouchard's books are solely his own and are not affiliated with the United States army.

ISBN: 978-1-4502-4152-6 (sc)
ISBN: 978-1-4502-4153-3 (hc)
ISBN: 978-1-4502-4154-0 (ebk)

Printed in the United States of America

iUniverse rev. date: 09/27/2012

Also by Paul Bouchard

Enlistment

The Boy Who Wanted to Be a Man

A Catholic Marries a Hindu

To the 2-142 INF (MECH) members who served at Guantanamo Bay, Cuba, in 2002 as part of the Enduring Freedom mission.

I'll Face You!

Paul Bouchard
July 2008

Acknowledgments

This is a work of fiction, but the background is real because I was there.

Back in 2002, I was a proud member of a Texas Army National Guard unit that came up on orders to Guantanamo Bay, Cuba, or Gitmo for short. Like most writers, I have to know what I write and write what I know, and it didn't take me too long to figure out that my observations and experiences during my Gitmo tour could be turned into a book. And that's just what I did—I wrote this novel about those Gitmo events and observations. I did take dramatic license with certain Gitmo events—sometimes I simply fabricated them; other times, I changed their time sequence because I was constantly asking the all-too-important what-if questions: *What if this had occurred? What if things had turned in this direction? What if I create this character?* In the end, any factual errors are my responsibility.

I'd like to thank the following individuals for helping me with this book:

Retired military officer, prolific writer, and ghost expert Ken Hudnall. Mr. Hudnall's expertise on ghosts was most helpful. His Web site, http://www.kenhudnall.com, was also invaluable.

Robert Barnsby and Charlie McElroy. Many writers have friends who review their manuscripts, and Rob and Charlie review mine. Their critical eyes always make them better.

Lastly, and most importantly, I wish to thank the squad members I served with—the members of Fifth Squad, First Platoon. More than anything, this is their story.

That damn package, man. I wish I would've never gotten that damn package.

—PFC Jerome Brown

CHAPTER 1

Jerome Brown took a sip from his full can of Coke. He was sitting on a wooden swivel stool, and he was visually scanning his sector. Suddenly, he started thinking about what he called his Big Four—four issues he devoted a lot of thought to, especially now, now that this was his last day at Gitmo.

Should I ETS in April? he thought. *Yeah, man, time to end the Army thing and return to civilian life.* ETS stood for "end term of service"—something at the very front of Brown's brain, for it was the first of his Big Four. He shrugged. *Yeah, National Guard's been good to me, but it's time to report to Fort Living Room civilian life.*

He took another sip of his ice-cold Coke as his second big issue—religion—came to mind. *Should I convert to Islam? Yeah, man, I think so. Many brothers do. I think I'm a go on that one.*

Tywanna, his girlfriend who lived back home in Lubbock, was the third of Brown's Big Four. Brown thought about her every day. *Should I pop the big question to T?* he thought as he kept scanning his sector. *I think so. Time for the big C—the big commitment. Tywanna's the girl for me, man. It's time to tie the knot.*

And then there was the last of his Big Four issues —something about a package Tywanna said she had sent him. Brown rubbed his chin as he thought about how Tywanna had e-mailed him three days earlier, saying she mailed him a package, sending it

DHL. *It's weird, man—this late in the game and T sends me a package? Wonder what that package is all 'bout.*

Brown was twenty-two years old and a landscape worker out of Lubbock, Texas. He was one of roughly 120 members of the 2-142, an Army National Guard unit (2-142 stands for Second Battalion, 142nd Infantry Mechanized) that was also based in Lubbock. Back in April of 2002, the 2-142 got activated— their mission: to guard Camp Delta, the detention facility at Guantanamo Bay, Cuba, which was housing the newly arriving Global War on Terrorism detainees. Now it was December of the same year, and the 2-142's six-month mission was on its last day, meaning Brown was on his last tower guard duty.

Brown was nearly six feet tall and tipped the scales at a portly 220 pounds. He stood up from his wooden swivel stool and stretched his legs. He was wearing his BDU uniform—the camouflaged battle dress uniform. He was also wearing a soft cap and black military boots.

He started pacing around his tower, Tower Three—a sturdy twelve-by-eight structure made of plywood. Suddenly he heard, "Attention all towers, attention all towers." The voice was emanating from his portable Saber radio, a radio that was standing erect on the floor next to the wooden stool. "This is the SOG. The time is oh two hundred hours. Commence radio checks in sequence at this time."

In three long strides, Brown reached his stool and picked up his Saber radio. He heard a strong voice, that of Ricardo Ruas, or Rosey, as he was called, say, "Tower Two."

With his right thumb, Brown pressed the radio's mike button and said, "Tower Three, good to go."

He released the button and heard, "Tower Four, Tower Five ...," all the way to the final tower.

Ah, seven more hours of this boring shit, he thought. *Then we got a few last-minute chores, and then we get on a chartered plane and head back to Texas. Yeah, man!*

He sat down on his wooden stool and took another sip of Coke.

"Good job, all towers," he heard loud and clear from the Saber radio. "Y'all stay vigilant on your last tower guard shift. SOG out."

Brown put down his Saber radio. *Good old Staff Sergeant Harrison's got sergeant of the guard duty tonight. Seems only right for our beloved squad leader to have our final shift.*

He shifted a bit on his stool to get himself comfortable, and then he resumed visually scanning his sector. It was 2:00 AM and dark out, but the Camp Delta compound was well lit, and off to the right, about a quarter mile away, Brown could clearly see Camp America, the small enclave of wooden cabins called hooches where Army soldiers like himself lived. Camp America was well lit as well, as was the dining facility, the Sea Galley, next to it. The Sea Galley was a Quonset hut composed of a thick white tarp hung over a metal frame.

Best I check on my TA-50 gear, man. He looked down to the left at the plywood floor, and there he saw his Kevlar helmet, M16 with magazine, pistol belt and two ammo pouches, two canteens, and his chemical mask.

My shit's good to go, he thought. And then, for no particular reason, he glanced to his right, and that's when he caught a glimpse of the graffiti written on one of the tower's plywood walls.

Shit, man, I've been on Tower Three before, but I forgot 'bout all the graffiti and shit on this tower.

The graffiti messages were scrawled on one of the tower's plywood walls. They were mostly written in ink—black or blue or red—but a few were written in gray pencil lead. He started reading the graffiti to himself:

Stop-loss sucks.
ETS=FREEDOM.
Someone kill the hard charger!
GITMO—the least worst place
I don't need Python pills—God gave me a BIG ONE.
Texas rules!
Twenty days and a wakeup
For a good time and a BJ, call Joe at 7236.

That was immediately followed by *Does Joe give good BJs?*

Below that, Brown read, *If God loved gays, he would've created Adam and Steve. Death to all fags!*

Brown read some more:

Jody got my bitch, but I'll get Jody when I return home.

Then carved in red ink was *666*, followed by *Jesus rules!*

And then the last graffiti message:

The real illegal immigrants came on the Mayflower.

What the hell, Brown thought. *I need to kill some time here on this boring-ass shift. Lemme think 'bout this graffiti crap.*

He thought about the first graffiti message: *Stop-loss sucks.*

Now there's a true fuckin' statement if I ever read one. Shit, I've got no regrets for signing up with the Texas Army National Guard. How long has it been? Over two years ago? But this stop-loss crap is really pushing me to get out of the Army when my ETS pops up next April.

He took a quick sip from his can of Coke, which he had placed on a thick wooden plank. The plank braced one of the tower's four supporting beam poles.

Fuckin' stop-loss, man. That's just a damn fuckin' way for politicians and the higher-up military brass to cover their asses and tell the public we don't have a recruiting problem. And it's also another way to avoid a draft, really.

Higher-ups say if you're in a critical MOS—military occupational specialty—or if your unit's really needed, then you can't get out of the Army, at least not now. That's a tough pill to swallow. Sign up with Uncle Sugar's Army for four years, and then your four years are over, and you think yous turning to good old Fort Living Room and civilian life, but right then Uncle Sugar says, "Oh no, soldier—I got your ass. I declare a stop-loss, and you can't get out right now 'cause the country needs you."

Brown suddenly thought about Congressman Charles Rangel. *Shit, man, when I think 'bout it, Brother Rangel is the shit with this crap. Rangel's my favorite politician, man,*

4

hands down. In my book, the brother should run for prez. Heck, Rangel says we need the draft, and he's probably right. Plus, I like Rangel's idea that a draft would level this unbalanced playing field; it would force rich kids to serve in the military too. That way it wouldn't be just the poor and the disadvantaged having to carry the load of fightin' Uncle Sugar's wars. That sounds like a plan to me. Brown pumped his fist. *Brother Rangel for prez, man.*

Brown stretched his thick neck by rotating it to the left and then to the right. He took another sip from his Coke can.

Fuck, man, whoever wrote that 'Stop-loss sucks' graffiti sure got it right. Me, I consider my black ass lucky 'cause no one's told us the 2-142 comes under a stop-loss. That's why when April comes 'round, I might just get out right then and there 'cause I ain't affected by no stop-loss, and I'm a lucky bitch my ETS is up.

He glanced down at the floor and shook his head in frustration. *Friggin' injustice, man. There's such a disconnect sometimes between the higher-ups and us dudes doing the grunt work. Politicians and higher-ups can just declare a stop-loss—the country needs you, blah, blah, blah. Fuck, man, how many of those higher-up high-class shits served in the military? Bush the prez, man—well, at least he did some time in the National Guard. Clinton, man, that dude was too busy having some fun with an intern and a cigar. Shit's fucked, in my opinion. That's injustice right there. Unfair written all over it. The politicians tell us we have an all-volunteer Army—my fat black ass we do.*

Brown slapped his ample bottom and then took another sip of Coke. *Why the fuck do we need stop-loss measures for anyway? Brother Rangel served in Korea. He's been through the real deal—brother knows what's up, what the true crappy and smelly shit tastes and smells like. That stop-loss crap does suck, and it's unfair. And even if Prez Bush served some, I bet anything his daughters won't serve a day in the military. Same story with Clinton's daughter.*

He looked at the next graffiti message: ETS=FREEDOM.

Yeah, that's true too, man. Again, my black ass is lucky on that one. Heck, the more I think 'bout it, the more I'm leaning toward returning to Fort Living Room and civilian life. Overall, I got no regrets joining Uncle Sugar's Army—hell, they's payin' for my college and shit. But that full twenty-year military career thing ... Nah, man, that shit ain't for me. Me, I'm looking forward to returning to civilian life 'cause the way I see it, four years of military service is enough. Yep, I'm leaning toward getting back to my job and getting my two-year associate's degree. I just gotta go to night class, that's all.

Brown ran his hand over the top of his head. He had everything worked out. After getting his associate's degree at the community college, he would transfer to Texas Tech in Lubbock and get his BA in criminal justice and sociology. *I dig that shit—sociology, politics, economics, the criminal justice system. That shit's real. Who knows, maybe someday I'll be a politician just like Brother Rangel. Get me a white-collar job; a necktie job. Anyway, that "ETS=FREEDOM" shit is the bomb, man—for real.*

Brown stood up and slowly walked to one of the four telephone polelike beams supporting Tower Three. He did that because his CamelBak was hanging from an old rusted nail driven into the beam. Taking his time, he gently placed the black nipple portion of the black tubing of the CamelBak in his mouth. He then turned the open valve and began to suck in some cool water.

Ah, that feels good. As much as Brown loved Coke, he knew it had a dehydrating effect on his body. He removed the CamelBak tube from his mouth, and then he turned the valve to the cutoff position and proceeded to sit back on the wooden swivel stool.

He looked at the next graffiti message: *Someone kill the hard charger!*

Another true statement right there. Hard-chargin' Captain Boswell. Dude's all high-speed and shit, but there's no secret why we call him the hard charger. Word is he pushed the higher-ups over in Austin to activate our unit. Don't know if any of that shit's for real, but it wouldn't surprise me any. Plus, I'm no fan of by-the-book Boswell.

Brown recalled being demoted by Boswell after getting into a fight with a Marine at the Windjammer Club. *Motherfucker busted me in rank. When was that … September? Yeah, back in September. Sure, I got out of hand, but that jarhead was looking at me funny. Friggin' jarhead started the shit too, but no—by-the-book Boswell didn't see it that way; he don't support his troops, man.* Brown mimicked Boswell, saying in a whiny voice, "I've got to set the example, Brown. Fighting will not be tolerated in this unit." Brown jabbed his finger toward the wall as he spoke, remembering the painful conversation in Boswell's quarters. "You're no longer a specialist, Brown. I'm busting you to private first class."

Sweet fuck, man. Higher-up disconnect once again right there. Shit, it's dudes like Boswell who got it all wrong—dudes like him don't give a rat's ass 'bout stop-losses.

He arched his back in order to stretch it, and then he interlaced his fingers and cracked his knuckles.

In my opinion, Prez Bush is another hard charger. I just hope Bush plans his shit straight in Kuwait and Saudi. Damn higher-ups—lots of power there. I forget who wrote that power is a great aphrodisiac, but whoever wrote that shit got it right. I just hope the prez and the other higher-ups don't get on some power trip; I hope they don't get too excited 'bout shit and fuck things up for the guys like me—guys with their boots on the ground.

Brown took a gulp from his Coke can; it was a gulp that made him swallow hard, cough two times, and belch. He took a few deep breaths. *Ah, that feels better.*

He placed his can of Coke on the flat wooden plank in front of him. He looked at the next graffiti message: *GITMO—the least worst place.*

Ah, that shit's all 'bout them T-shirts for sale over at the Navy Exchange. Some dude came up with that saying for the T-shirts, and now 'em shirts are selling pretty solid.

He quickly looked at the next message: *I don't need Python pills—God gave me a* BIG ONE.

Brown smiled. *Heck, that's some dude writing 'bout Specialist Juan Lopez, the one and only Johnny Python. Friggin' Python, man. That dude's been chasing pussy here ever since we hit the ground back in June. Dude's all wild and open 'bout his shit too. Hell, I couldn't believe it when he told us his wife—his own wife, man—sent him these Python pills and horny goat weed shit to make his stick harder. Talk 'bout an open marriage. And his Python pills and horny goat weed are on that little wooden plank directly above his cot back in our hooch—all out in the open for us Fifth Squadders to see. Python's always chasing pussy wherever and whenever he can: Windjammer Club, Tiki Bar, bowling alley, movie theater, Windmill Beach. Wherever there's chicks, Python's chasing 'em and asking 'em for dates and shit.*

Brown took another sip of Coke. *Shit, that reminds me— the chick situation here's a real tough nut to crack. Not that that's an issue with me 'cause I'm tight and loyal with my Tywanna, but I know there ain't much in the chick department here at Gitmo. Shit, there's a saying here at Gitmo: "Get more at Gitmo," but everybody knows it ain't true 'cause there's so few chicks here. Like in our unit, man. None of the girls in the 2-142 came to this Gitmo mission 'cause this here is considered an infantry mission, and women ain't allowed in the infantry.* Brown suddenly thought about the unit from the Mississippi National Guard, the unit that was over at Camp America. That unit had some women because they were MPs, and women were allowed to be MPs. The women worked inside Camp Delta, which was better duty, Brown felt, than what his unit was doing—pulling boring shifts in the towers and at vehicle checkpoints.

Shit, man, Python's always asking those female Mississippi MPs out on dates. Also the Marine, Navy, and Air Force chicks—he asks them for dates too. I've noticed when I'm out drinking beer or shooting pool at the Windjammer Club that 'em chicks stick to their own branch: Marine chick jarheads stick with Marine dude jarheads; Navy chick squids stick with Navy dude squids; Air Force chick zoomies stick with Air Force dude zoomies. That's just the way it is, man. For real.

Brown cracked his knuckles, and then he extended his legs to stretch them. He looked at the next graffiti message: *Texas rules!*

Amen to that, brother. Lone Star State's where it's at. I just hope our former governor turned commander in chief, Prez Bush, knows what he's doing with that troop buildup in Kuwait and Saudi.

Brown looked at the next message: *Twenty days and a wakeup.*

Shit, man, that was written by some dude who had twenty-one days left here. Twenty days and a wakeup. Heck, it's now wake up, do our last shift, pack, and get the hell outta this "least worst place" called Gitmo. Them twenty days are past, man. Last day is today. Six months in this hot, humid place is long enough.

He looked at the next messages: *For a good time and a BJ, call Joe at 7236. Does Joe give good BJs? If God loved gays, he would've created Adam and Steve. Death to all fags!*

Well, well, thought Brown as he kept scanning his Tower Three sector. *Heck, Prez Clinton's don't ask, don't tell policy still rules, so we got to let the gay brothers be. Shit don't bother me none, really. You's queer, you's queer—what can I say?*

Brown cast his eyes downward. *Then again, I'm thinking of converting to Islam, and some of my Muslim buds told me Islam don't look too favorably on that homo stuff. Same thing with booze and credit cards, man—Muslims ain't supposed to do none of that shit. But Islam speaks to me, man. It's got nothing to do with the Muslim detainees here at Gitmo. Shit, I've been thinking 'bout converting to Islam ever since my buddy Otis got out of the slammer and told me he found Islam. Bottom line—Islam's got some good stuff: one god, pray, do good, help the poor. That's Islam right there. Plus, it's really the religion for people of color. Cassius Clay found it and became Muhammad Ali. Malcolm X found it too. I like some of Malcolm*

X's shit, especially his message 'bout blacks needing to feel better 'bout themselves and being more self-reliant and shit. Dr. King, man ... well, he's the big hero, the Big Dog. I know he wasn't a Muslim, but he's still dah man.

Brown sipped from his Coke can. *Shit, I know some of the Islam the brothers find in prison preaches some "hate whitey" crap and "hate Jews" crap, but I don't buy into that shit.* Brown thought about his boss back home, Mr. Reichman, who owned the landscaping business he worked for. *That dude's Jewish, and I get along great with him. He's loaded—he owns a construction company, the landscaping business, and tons of real estate. He treats me real well.*

Brown thought about the time that Reichman offered him a foreman position. The promotion meant more hours, though, which Brown couldn't swing because he was taking college courses at night. *That's when Mr. Reichman told me to concentrate on school. He also told me he'd consider me for a property manager job on one of his developments once I graduated. So I ain't got nothin' against Jews. Mama, she'll be disappointed with me converting to Islam 'cause she's a devout Baptist and all, but she'll turn ' round; I know she will.*

Brown quickly shifted on the stool to get more comfortable.

What was I thinking 'bout? Oh yeah, homo shit. Well, that shit don't bother me any. I think I can be Muslim and have no problem with gays. Booze, credit cards ... oh, and no pork. Muslims ain't supposed to eat pork. That'll be tough: no beer, no plastic, no eating pork, but the gay thing I can handle.

He stretched his neck again, and then he looked at the next graffiti message: *Jody got my bitch, but I'll get Jody when I return home.*

Shit, man, that Jody crap must bite royally. Gone on deployment, then this Jody dude gets your woman—that's what that saying's all 'bout.

Brown stood up to stretch. He started pacing around the tower floor. He peered at the next two messages: *666* and *Jesus rules!*

He sat back down on the wooden swivel stool.

Friggin' devil-worshipping fucks. Never know 'bout them dudes; they's missing something in the head. Couple screws loose—better yet, couple screws missing. All I can do on my end is hope and pray those twisted fucks find God, find Allah, man. As for "Jesus rules!"— ain't nothing wrong with that. Jesus is mentioned in the Koran—I know 'cause I'm reading the Koran on the side every other day or so, whenever I'm off shift.

Brown quickly looked at the last message: *The real illegal immigrants came on the Mayflower.*

I don't agree with that one. Shit, if the descendents of them Mayflower Pilgrims hadn't imported slaves, me and my ancestors would still be struggling in Africa and shit. Not that I've been to Africa, but everything I've heard and read says the place ain't all that great. Human migration, man— shit happens; shit's natural. Ain't nothing wrong with them Pilgrims leaving for religious freedom.

Suddenly, Brown heard the voice again over his radio: "Attention, all towers, attention, all towers. This is the SOG. Commence radio checks in sequence at this time."

Brown picked up his Saber radio and called in his radio check to Staff Sergeant Harrison. He then glanced at his watch and saw that it was 0300. *Fuck, man, I've got six hours left on this shift.*

CHAPTER 2

Yolita Banks raised three kids on her own. She was fifteen when she had her first child, a boy she named Keyshawn. At seventeen, she had a girl she named Tonya; Yolita gave birth to another girl, Tywanna, at nineteen.

Keyshawn never knew his biological father—the man who had impregnated Yolita left soon after Keyshawn's birth, never to return. Tonya and Tywanna, however, both knew who their dad was. His name was Charles Banks.

Originally from Louisiana, Charles Banks had found work for a taxicab company in Amarillo, Texas, and it was there that he had met the attractive Yolita. The couple never did marry, but Yolita took on her beau's surname nonetheless.

Banks loved life and lived it to the fullest. He had many loves: Yolita and the kids, blues and jazz, fine clothes when he could afford them, booze, gambling, and other women. Yolita knew about these loves, including the latter, and continually forgave him for what she called his "bad habits," his "temptations."

Of these "bad habits," Banks' gambling habit proved to be his downfall. His love of gambling brought him crushing debts—debts so bad he had to borrow more and more just to stay afloat. When one of these gambling debts went unpaid for too long, a loan shark had apparently had enough of Banks' excuses and took action. Banks' lifeless body was discovered in a cotton field some eighty miles south of Amarillo. That had been eight years ago, in 1994. Luckily, the family of four—Yolita and her three children—qualified for food stamps and Section 8 housing soon after Charles's untimely death.

As for Keyshawn, he quit high school when he was sixteen, but he did obtain his GED by the time he reached nineteen. He then did a two-year stint in the Air Force, after which he returned to Amarillo, moved in with his girlfriend, and started his own auto detailing business.

Then there were Tonya and Tywanna, now twenty-one and nineteen, respectively. Tywanna, a beautician student and part-time salesperson at a women's clothing store, was dating Jerome Brown. Two and a half years earlier, when she was seventeen and a high school senior, Tywanna gave birth to a healthy eight-pound baby she named Danielle. Danielle's father, Roy Peterson, was a former Amarillo High School football star who had his college football career cut short by frequent knee operations. Long out of the picture when it came to Danielle, Peterson was last heard from in 2001. He had gone to Oklahoma City and was working odd jobs and coaching youth football there. No phone calls, birthday or Christmas gifts, or child support payments ever came from Peterson.

Tonya, two years senior to Tywanna, worked as a cashier at an Amarillo Super Wal-Mart. She too was dating, but it wasn't anything serious or steady like what Tywanna had with Jerome. And that—the fact that she wasn't going steady—was a problem for Tonya. In fact, Tonya was full of problems.

For starters, Tonya suffered from depression and anxiety attacks. Her self-esteem, her self-confidence—essentially her entire outlook on herself and on life in general—was shaky. Very shaky. Tonya was a pessimist about all things. Her mood swings were extremely volatile, and she was jealous too, especially of her younger sister. No matter what she did or how hard she tried, Tonya could never keep up with Tywanna's successes.

Take, for example, looks. While Tonya could be described as "okay looking," Tywanna, without question, was an absolute beauty by anyone's standards. She was tall and slender with curves in all the right places. Her skin was smooth and silky, the color of mocha. She laughed easily, showing off her stunning white teeth and luscious lips. And her gorgeous brown eyes were the stuff of poetry. In short, she was a hottie, a nice catch, a girl who didn't have to struggle to get dates because she was always in demand.

Then there was athletics—yet another area where Tonya couldn't match her younger sister, Tywanna. Back in high school, Tonya tried out for just about every sport. Sometimes she made the tryout cut, but sometimes she didn't, and when she did make the cut, the most she could aspire to was assuming the role of a bench-warming substitute player. Tywanna, on the other hand, lettered four years in a row in both swimming and track, and she was the cocaptain of the ever-popular cheerleading squad.

Tonya was also jealous of Tywanna's status as a mother. Tywanna had a cute baby, Danielle. Having a cute baby, being a mother—Tonya was jealous that Tywanna had those things while she did not. And to add more salt to the wound, more pain to the loser attitude, Tonya had actually been impregnated in 2001, but, unfortunately, miscarried. The discouraged Tonya had locked herself in her bedroom for two straight weeks after that devastating loss.

And Tonya's mean streak was yet another problem area. The way Tonya saw it, "correcting wrongs," "leveling the playing field," and "getting even" were all things she was good at because that's where her manipulative skills could and often did kick in. Bottom line: Tonya's strategy was always to find a person's weakness. She was always looking for a perceived enemy's weak spot in order to exploit the fuck out of it.

Sitting on her mother's old blue felt sofa, which was donated by a local Salvation Army store, Tonya's malicious and manipulative mind went to work. It was mid-November of 2002, and it was cold out that day in Amarillo, so much so that Tonya was wearing a thick sweater over a thick sweatshirt in the ill-heated Section 8 home. She came up with a plan.

Tywanna's weakness is guys, she thought, smirking. *Guys are always chasing her. She's loyal to Jerome right now, but I be testing her.*

CHAPTER 3

W arm and muggy. Brown sat on the wooden swivel stool of Tower Three, visually scanning his sector, which meant he was mostly staring at darkness because it was still the early morning hours. *Man, this tower guard shit is boring*, he thought. *Six more hours of this crap.*

He took a sip from his Coke can. *Wonder what's in that package Tywanna sent me. She hasn't sent me a thing during this whole deployment, but with just a week left, she sends me a package? Hmm. And that package better come in this morning when I get off shift. Damn good thing T sent it DHL.*

He did a few shoulder shrugs as he kept scanning his sector, thinking back to the good time he had in October when he was on leave. *Sure was nice seeing Tywanna and Danielle up in Amarillo. I'm cool with her mom too. I know Yolita likes me, man. She told me so. Said, "Jerome, you bettah than those other boys chasin' my Tywanna, and I know you're real good with Danielle too." Ten days of leave—it was great.*

He was staring at the pitch-black sky directly in front of him. He quickly glanced at his M16 and TA-50 gear to make sure they were good to go.

Yeah, it was fun in Amarillo back in October. 'Course it took me a full day to get up there and then another full day to return to Gitmo, so it was eight days of vacation, not ten. Had a good time—going to the mall, eating out all the time, getting DVDs at Blockbuster and watching them at Tywanna's. I blew a lot of dough, but that's expected. Food, DVDs, trips to the mall, even the gas for Yolita's old car—shit adds up, man, but it was worth every penny. And spending time with Danielle— that too was cool. I love that little girl.

An image suddenly popped into Brown's mind. He remembered shopping with Tywanna and Danielle at the mall in Amarillo. Danielle was in her stroller, struggling with the chocolate ice cream cone that was half on her face, neck, and chest. They were window-shopping at a jewelry store. Brown was checking out some watches.

Shit, that's it! Maybe that's what Tywanna sent me in that package. I was checking out those nice used Rolexes. I was thinking of buying one but really couldn't swing the twelve-hundred-dollar price tag—not with all the money I was already spending and not with the holidays being 'round the corner. Heck, I remember Tywanna seeing me eye one particular Rolex, and that's when she told me, "Jerome, baby, if I can come up with the money, I'll buy you that watch."

Yeah, man, maybe that's what T sent me in that package. Brown smiled, taking another sip of Coke. *Yeah, bet anything the package is that used Rolex I wanted.*

He smiled again. He then decided to look inside Camp Delta. *There they are, the detainees,* he thought. *They's sleeping in their small cells. Heck, I know some of my 2-142 buddies think I've been wrestling with this whole Islam conversion thing 'cause I'm here at Gitmo ... and I somehow identify with these detainees. But that ain't it. Shit, I've been thinking 'bout becoming a Muslim some two years now, basically ever since Otis got out of the slammer. Otis did some mighty hard time behind bars, but one thing that turned him 'round was Islam. Then Otis got me interested in it: submit to Allah, help the poor, live a clean life. Shit appeals to me, man.*

Brown thought more about the detainees in their cells. *It's amazin' what the media's saying 'bout this Gitmo place. Heck, I check my Yahoo! e-mail account daily, and there always seems to be some headline story 'bout Gitmo and the detainees here. Shit, from where I sit, I see and know quite a bit 'bout this place. I know the detainees here are well fed, that's for sure. I also know they ain't fed pork 'cause Muslims ain't supposed to eat pork products. Heck, I remember Boswell telling us Fifth Squadders that the typical detainee here at Gitmo gains something like twelve pounds. I also know each detainee here is given the Koran and prayer time. Sure, the holding cells here at Camp Delta are small, and yeah, the reports 'bout detainees' heads being shaved are true, but that's 'cause lots of the detainees have lice, man. At least that's what one MP told me back in July—that the detainees have lice, so shaving their heads is a health and safety thing. So is the mandatory TB test 'cause some of these detainees have TB. I also know the detainees get good medical and dental care here.*

Brown removed his soft cap to scratch the top of his head. He rubbed his eyes and nose, and then he yawned. He looked at his old black Timex strapped around his left wrist. It read 3:26.

God, another five and a half hours of this shit. Hmm, where was I? Oh, the detainees. Brown thought about what fellow Fifth Squadder Bouchey—a law student—had told him about detainees and their rights. Bouchey felt that the detainees should eventually be charged with something and given their day in court. *Bouchey also told me each detainee should have a lawyer to represent 'em and shit. So the legal rights stuff— which interests me 'cause I dig that shit—is a bit iffy.*

Brown spun himself around and grabbed his Coke can from the nearby wooden plank. He took a quick sip from it, and then he turned around again to look inside Camp Delta.

Most of the detainees here are young dark-skinned Muslims. Some are blacks from Africa, and some are Asians, but most are Muslims from Afghanistan. Most are hairy too, and a good number of them have full beards. A few detainees here are old too. One guy here is like in his seventies and shit. I think there's a few youngsters here too, like sixteen-year-olds and shit. What else, man, 'bout these detainees? Well, a good number of them are amputees—missing arms and legs and shit.

Brown glanced down at his M16 and TA-50 gear. He then looked out, slightly to his right, about a quarter mile away, at Camp America.

Hmm … Wonder where our hooch is. The Fifth Squad hooch. Hooch 1305. It's next to the computer center hooch … yeah, that's it. Right there. I can't see it all, but I can see the roof of our hooch.

Where was I? Oh yeah, the detainees. Shit, why the detainees went on a hunger strike back in September beats me. MPs handled it well. Nothing came of it, thank God. I think the whole thing lasted a day or so.

Brown took a quick sip of Coke.

Man, that gets me thinkin' 'bout our MPs here. 'Em dudes have it tough. Lots of 'em get stop-lossed, and a good number of 'em get water and urine and even feces thrown at 'em by some of these detainees. Glad I don't have to deal with that shit.

Brown stood up. He stretched his arms above his head, and then he yawned.

Last shift. Can't wait to get back to Fort Hood, Texas, deactivate over there, and then head back to Lubbock.

He started pacing around Tower Three.

What else can I do to kill time? What else can I think 'bout?

He looked to the west and saw Tower One and Tower Two. A thought occurred to him. He decided to think of his fellow battle buddies, his fellow Fifth Squadders on tower guard. He walked back to the stool and took a seat. He thought about his buddies based on their cot layout back at the hooch.

First cot—directly to the right as you enter hooch 1305 from the front entrance—is Staff Sergeant Whitcomb's cot. Now there's one squared-away soldier if I ever knew one. Heck, I think Whitcomb's the best soldier, the best noncommissioned officer, in our platoon.

First Platoon, man. We rock. Third Platoon? Those dudes from the Valley sure get in trouble and like to fight. They's always fighting, man, even amongst themselves. Got some good dudes in that platoon, but lots of 'em get in trouble and shit. Brown thought about Second Platoon too. *Those dudes weren't any better. They was always on restriction because they's always getting into trouble.*

Anyway, I think Whitcomb's the best of the best. Cream of the crop right there. He's strong and built -- there's no fat on that dude. Heck, he and Bouchey tied for the highest PT score back in September. He told me he's from Wyoming. He also told me he's divorced and has a kid, a little boy. I know he moved to Texas 'cause he got a job with a Tyco subsidiary.

Brown thought about Tyco. *Shit, man, I'm glad I read the news—I know what's going on. Corporate greed, man, that's what's going on. Friggin' CEO of Tyco spent hard-earned company money on his pricey New York City digs. Then he turned 'round and spent corporate funds on some big birthday bash for his wife. Friggin' company's struggling 'cause all them higher-ups are livin' in hog heaven. Shit ain't right, man, and Whitcomb don't tolerate that crap. Heck, Whitcomb told me not too long ago that he still has his job when he returns home, but he worries 'bout the future of Tyco.*

Corporate greed, that's all it is. It's all 'bout the golden rule—he who has the gold rules. That's it right there in a nutshell. Heck, what we need to do is give all the gold to the poor people, man. That's what I believe. Brother Rangel would back me up on that one.

Brown took a quick sip from his Coke can. The drink was now warm, but he didn't care. *What else 'bout Whitcomb? Hmm ... Well, he got promoted to staff sergeant back in August. That was a good promotion. He deserved it.*

Brown thought about other promotions in his unit. He hated that a lot of fuckups in his unit got promoted. Dudes who couldn't pass their physical fitness (PT) test got promoted. *Wasn't fair.* Dudes even got promoted who didn't want to attend the professional leadership development course (PLDC) required to make sergeant. Brown hated that. *Heck, that's another one of the hard charger's problems—too soft on promotions, man.*

Course with me, Captain Boswell did the opposite—he friggin' demoted my ass. "I have to set an example, Brown," he said. Heck, other 2-142 GIs got into fights. Yeah, they didn't fight a Marine jarhead, but still. Injustice. That's what that is right there.

Brown pondered for a second or two. *What else 'bout squared-away Whitcomb? Well, he chews tobacco ... I know that. Shit, one time Whitcomb told a group of us Fifth Squadders that in high school in Wyoming the teachers let the students chew tobacco in class. For real. Put some snuff in your mouth and chew away, all while attending classes. Wyoming, man. That's cool shit right there.*

Brown reached for his top left BDU pocket with his right hand. He reached inside and pulled out a small packet of Trident gum. In seconds he was chewing gum while still scanning his sector.

That's 'bout it for Whitcomb. Who's next? Next cot's Sergeant Bouchey's—the Texas Tech law student dude. Bouchey's cool. He likes reading a lot and writing too. Also jogging.

Heck, just a couple of weeks ago, Bouchey told us Fifth Squadders he hopes to get picked up by the Army JAG Corps once he finishes law school. He said he hopes to become a published writer someday. It was Bouchey who introduced me to John Grisham books. "If you like to read, Brown, you'll like John Grisham novels. He's a real good writer," he told me not too long ago. In fact, Bouchey went down to the Navy Exchange store and bought me a copy of Grisham's Skipping Christmas. *Bouchey even signed the inside cover of it. I remember it very well.*

He had written:
To a future Charles Rangel.
Best of luck with your college plans.
Merry Christmas,
I'll Face You!
Bouchey

That was cool of Bouchey. I liked the book too. "I'll Face You!" is our unit's motto. Shit's a cool motto, man—I'll Face You!

Brown thought more about Bouchey as he chewed gum and visually scanned his sector. *Bouchey's divorced, just like Whitcomb. He told me he also got a girlfriend stateside, like Whitcomb. Bouchey likes Jack Nicholson. Does a pretty good imitation of him too. His favorite movie is* A Few Good Men, *with Nicholson as that Marine colonel right here at Gitmo. Bouchey loves that movie, man, and he can quote from it.*

Thinking about *A Few Good Men* made Brown remember something else Bouchey told the Fifth Squadders awhile back. It was an incident related to the Cuban fence line at Gitmo. It happened when Bouchey and Vega were working an observation point. They saw a Cuban soldier toss a football over the fence to an American Marine. He remembered Bouchey saying, *Things can't be too bad here when opposing military men are tossing a football to one another.*

'Course that's when I told Bouchey the Cubans had land mines on their side of the fence to prevent their people from escaping to American safety. "Good point," I remember Bouchey telling me.

Brown then remembered Bouchey telling the Fifth Squadders about some World War I stuff. *Bouchey said that the British and the opposing Germans sometimes took breaks from the fighting and played soccer against one another.*

That's Bouchey, man—talking 'bout politics and history and shit. I like that. Heck, he's one of a handful of 2-142 dudes who know something 'bout politicians like Charles Rangel. Law student Bouchey's having a field day here at Gitmo with all this politics and detainee stuff—stuff like the Constitution, POW status, the Geneva Conventions. Bouchey's all over that shit, and I like it when he talks 'bout it.

Brown spun around a full 360 degrees on his swivel stool to break the monotony. He kept chewing gum, and then he resumed scanning his sector.

Next cot ... that would be Juan Lopez, better known as the one and only Johnny Python. Dude's friggin' nuts, man. Python pill popping, horny goat weed takin' ... all in the hopes of having a bigger one and getting dates. Chicks—that's all Python thinks 'bout, 24/7. His radar screen's always on the lookout for babes. "Sue's working night shift at Delta, so I'll ask her out on Friday when she's off; Lolly Pop's working the day shift, and she's off Wednesday, so I'll ask her out then ..."

Brown raised an eyebrow. It was okay to think about that shit, but to talk openly about it was another thing. *Heck, he's always telling us Fifth Squadders what his pussy-chasing game plan is.* Brown remembered Python showing the Fifth Squadders letters he wrote to women listed in dating services magazines. *'Course, he then proudly tacks the letters he receives from them to the wall next to his cot. Shit, man, the whole thing's a money gimmick in my opinion—'cause Python has to pay to get the addresses from the magazines.*

Brown kept scanning his sector while chewing gum.

Back in July, Python rented a car even though the bus service at Gitmo wasn't bad. Buses could take the guys anywhere they needed to go: the bowling alley, the Windjammer Club, the Tiki Bar, the gym, McDonald's, the Navy Exchange store, and the free movie theater. *Everywhere, man. 'Course the bus ain't good enough for ladies' man Python—I guess the bus ain't fast enough, and he don't like to wait in line. That's why he rented himself a car.*

Brown recalled some of Python's pickup lines when Python was cruisin' in his car: *"Hey, need a lift?"or "Where you heading, sweet honey?" or "I'm headin' that way anyway. Why don't I give you a lift?"* At least, that was what Martin, nicknamed Mini Me, had told the Fifth Squadders. Mini Me hung out with Python.

Shit, man, Brown thought. *We named him Mini Me 'cause he looks like Python except he's shorter. 'Em two are always cruisin' 'round together. Mini Me, he just tags along, man—he's happily married and ain't foolin' 'round here. But Python, he don't stop at nothing to get dates. Shit, he even tries to pick up chicks when he's working the vehicle checkpoints.*

Brown thought about another Python pickup line: "Hi, honey. What you doing tonight? How's 'bout some drinks at the Windjammer Club? My treat—promise." He then thought about how Python carried a cheap camera with him to take photos of chicks.

Gotta give Python an A for effort, man. Full-blown letter-writing campaign, his car rental angle, and taking photos with chicks. Dude's got all the bases covered. Funny thing, though -- most of us Fifth Squadders doubt Python's getting any. Not that he's a bad-looking dude or anything. Dates—sure, man, he gets those now and then. But scoring? I've got my doubts.

Staff Sergeant Harrison came to mind. *Now Harrison, on the other hand, that brother's got a muscular bod, fine clothes, the smooth dancin' moves. And I know many of 'em white chicks dig the black man. Bet anything Harrison's been scoring down here at Gitmo even if the chick-to-dick ratio is something like ten to one or some shit like that.*

Brown slowly twisted his neck to stretch it. *What else 'bout Python? Oh yeah, how the hell could I forget? Dude fucked up royally just a few days ago. Got busted for a DUI. Story I heard was Python got off work and headed straight for his Pussy Mobile. He drove to the Windjammer Club and started having a few cold ones.* Brown knew there wasn't anything wrong with having a few beers; the guys were allowed to drink at Gitmo as long as they didn't drink twelve hours before going on shift.

But the problem for Python was that someone in our squad had to go on sick call, and that fucked up our whole work schedule 'cause instead of Python going on shift at noon, he had to report to work at 6:00 AM. 'Course Python had a few too many brewskies, but he still tried to drive back in time for work. Shit didn't happen, man. His Python Mobile got into a fender bender with a Humvee driven by a bunch of jarheads.

The Navy police had showed up, and they had done a full police report. Whitcomb later told Brown that Python had to do a Breathalyzer test, count backward, walk in a straight line, and touch his nose. *'Course Python bo-lowed these tests and got hit with a DUI. Right now, I think Python's got some Army JAG lawyer working his case. Court date's in early January, and 'cause of that, Python won't be comin' on our chartered plane later today. Poor Python. I feel bad for the dude; he won't be home for the holidays.*

Brown stood up. He interlaced his fingers, cracked his knuckles, and stared at the dark sky to the south. Only his gum kept him company.

Bet anything Tywanna sent me that Rolex 'cause— He suddenly heard *cling clang cling* and knew someone was heading up the metal ladder to his tower. He walked over to the tower entrance and peeked down. He saw a soldier in full battle rattle: Kevlar helmet, M16 slung over the shoulder, TA-50 gear, and CamelBak hugging his back.

"Who's that, man?" Brown called. He couldn't quite make out who it was. "That you, Vega?"

"Roger that," Vega said as he struggled up the ladder rungs. Vega produced more *cling clang cling* sounds as his M16 hit the metal ladder rungs and guardrails encircling the tower ladder.

Brown reached out with his right hand to help Vega onto the tower floor. "Thanks, Brown," Vega said. "I hate climbing that ladder with all my gear on." Brown wasn't surprised that Vega was having trouble because Vega was overweight by twenty pounds and didn't work out at the gym like most of the Fifth Squadders.

"I hear you, bud," said Brown as he released Vega's hand. "What up?"

"Papa Smurf has got me checking the towers—that is all," Vega said in his Spanish accent. "Commo good?" he asked, referring to whether Brown's communications equipment was good to go. "Need batteries or anything?"

"Nah, man, shit's cool. I'm good to go. Have a seat, Vega."

"Thank you," Vega said, smiling, showing his gold front tooth. He put down his M16, removed his helmet and his gear, and sat on the big plastic footlocker located near the center of the tower. As he sat, he heaved a big sigh of relief.

"You see, Brown, Papa Smurf came to my tower," said Vega. "I'm on Tower Six tonight, and Papa Smurf was doing his tower checks, but then he decided to pull my shift for an hour. He wants me to check on some of the other towers. I am sure his knees are hurting him. He doesn't like climbing ladders."

"I see," said Brown, nodding in approval while he sat on his wooden swivel stool.

"You know, Brown, I think Papa Smurf's getting too old for this infantry stuff."

Brown smiled. "Yeah. Good old Sergeant First Class Rivera. Heck, I heard he was in Vietnam, man."

"Yes, yes, he was," Vega said as he proceeded to grab his CamelBak black tube and insert it in his mouth. He took a big gulp of water. "Yes, I think Papa Smurf is like ... oh ... he's more than fifty years old."

Brown changed the subject. "Can you believe it, bro? Later today we're on a plane headin' to Texas. We'll be back at Fort Hood tonight, Vega."

"I can't wait," responded Vega. "Six months here is long enough."

"Not much of a mission, really. What ya think, Vega? Detainees can't escape from this motherfuckin' Camp Delta joint. And Castro ain't gonna attack us—dude's fucked up, but he ain't that stupid."

"Well, Brown, I know it's been boring here, but you cannot trust the Communists," said Vega. "Castro and Communists you can never trust, no? This I know, my friend, because I grew up in a Communist country, Nicaragua."

"Yeah, I heard 'bout that shit," said Brown. "I remember reading 'bout that somewhere."

"Yes, Communists messed up everything in my country of birth. When I was a little boy, the Communists took over. The police would run around everywhere and talk about how we needed to help the poor. Brown, my friend, I tell you this. I had this uncle in Nicaragua. He worked very hard. It happened that he owned two houses. You know what the Communists did?"

"Nah, bro," said Brown as he kept scanning his sector. His back was to Vega. "What they do, man?"

"They seized one of his houses, that's what they did." Vega moved his arms and hands as he spoke passionately. "They went to my uncle and said, 'We have a lot of poor people, and you have two houses. We are taking one of your houses and giving it to the poor.'"

"Well, I'm all for helping the poor," said Brown, scratching his forehead and rubbing his eyes. "Especially in this age of corporate greed and all. But shit, man, I dunno 'bout seizing property and shit. That's fucked, man."

"That is the Communists for you, Brown—you can never trust them."

"Well, maybe," said Brown, "but Castro ain't got nothin' on us, brother. We's way too big for his ass."

"Yes, you are correct, my friend," Vega said. He shifted a bit on the footlocker. "But I fear the Communists precisely because they fear us. They operate out of fear, my friend—this I know. There is a word I am thinking of … what is the word I am looking for? … ah, paranoid. Paranoid, Brown. The Communists are paranoid."

"How so?"

"Oh, Brown, the Communists are always paranoid. Let me tell you a story, my friend. It is the story of how I came to this great country, the United States." Vega cleared his throat. "Our family has been blessed, Brown. You see, my father, thank God, was a commercial fisherman in Nicaragua. Me and my sister didn't see my father a lot because he was often far away on the ocean, but my father made good money by standards of Nicaragua—and my father, as a commercial fisherman, saw nice places, especially in the United States. New Orleans, Miami, Baltimore, New York City. My father saw things, Brown."

"That's interesting, man," said Brown. "That's good shit right there."

"Yes, yes, it is," said Vega. He continued, "Well, my friend, I remember once when my dear father bought me and my sister a nice new red fire truck from the United States—you know, a children's fire truck with two seats and pedals so the children can drive it."

"Yeah, I know what you talkin' 'bout, buddy."

"Yes, well, my sister and I loved the new fire truck, Brown. It was the best gift I ever had. I remember me and my sister loved to pedal the fire truck up and down the narrow street where we lived in Nicaragua. It was a beautiful truck, Brown. It had a nice little fire bell on it too. My sister loved to ring the nice little fire bell. Kids on our street would watch us pedal by. They would wave at us, Brown. It was a beautiful gift."

"That's cool," said Brown.

"Yes, and you know what happened? I think we had the beautiful fire truck for three weeks, and that is when one of these Communist government workers came knocking on our door. My father was not home because he was out at sea, but my mother, me and my sister, and my grandmother—who lived with us—were at home. I remember the government worker interviewing my dear mother. He asked her, 'Where did this children's fire truck come from?'"

"What did she say, man?"

"My mother did not lie. She told him my father was a commercial fisherman and that because of his work, he sometimes stops at ports. She told him my father bought the fire truck for me and my sister and that the truck was bought in Boston. And that, my friend, is when the Communist government worker said, 'Oh, your husband must be working for the CIA. Only a CIA agent on the Yankee payroll could afford such a toy. Our Communist government will be closely observing your family, Ms. Vega.'"

"For real, man?" said Brown. He quickly spun his stool around to face Vega. "Dude thought your father was CIA and shit."

"Yes. That is how the Communists think and operate, my friend. They are paranoid; they are scared. They operate out of fear."

"Shit's fucked, man."

"Yes, it is. Well, anyway, my father left Nicaragua shortly after the Communists took over. I think he wanted to live in Miami, but he ended up in New York City. He started as a dishwasher."

"Shit, that's rough duty, man," Brown said.

"Then the United States started giving visas to reunify families. Canada, the United Kingdom, and Australia I think were also giving visas, but we decided to live in the United States."

"I see," said Brown. "That's cool shit right there—giving visas and shit."

Vega nodded. "Anything to escape the paranoid Communists." He looked down at the plywood floor. "Brown, my friend, my family got a visa to enter the United States. We reunited with my father, and we ended up in Texas. It is true we were first on welfare, but after about eighteen months, my father and mother found jobs."

"That's cool," Brown said. "What did you do next?"

"Me, I started speaking English right away in school. I was thirteen. My sister was eleven when we arrived, and she too started learning English right away. Today, my parents live in California, where my dear father is a preacher. Thank God for the United States, my friend. This is a great country."

"Yeah, man, that's cool," said Brown. "I'm glad things worked out for you and your family."

"Me too," said Vega. Then he added, "And now, my friend, you see why I don't trust the Communists. And with Castro being on our tail here, one never knows. Maybe he will be stupid and decide to attack us."

Brown said, "Man, I doubt it. We's too powerful for his ass."

"That is true, but one never knows because Communists are always paranoid. That is why they have mines on their side of the Cuban fence line—to prevent their own people from escaping the Communist regime. Communists operate out of fear, Brown."

"Yeah, I see that. Shit's all jacked up."

"Yes, yes, it is."

A few quiet seconds passed. At one point, Brown spit his Trident gum into his right hand and threw the gum in the black plastic garbage bag lying next to his TA-50 gear.

"Vega, do you know 'bout a few of the Cubans who made it through the fence line? Remember what Captain Boswell told us a couple months ago? How some Cuban colonel made it through and ended up at the Navy Exchange store?"

"Yes, my friend, I remember," said Vega. "The Cuban colonel risked his life to make it to Gitmo and American soil. He was lucky, Brown. The fact there are mines on the Cuban side is real—this I know because I remember when Nelson, over in Second Platoon, once told me he was on observation duty one afternoon. He was doing his job—looking at the Cuban fence line from far away up on the hill—and he told me he saw a deer get a leg blown off because it stepped on a Cuban mine. Poor animal ... one of God's creatures."

"That's too bad," said Brown as he stood up to stretch.

Vega, still sitting, said, "The Communists build walls and fences and place mines to keep their people in. I tell you this: whenever Castro and the Communists lose power in Cuba—and I pray to God they do—then I know floods of Cubans will migrate to Miami."

"Many already have, man," said Brown. He sat back on his stool.

"Yes, but more will come. Living under Communism sucks, Brown. There will be a power struggle in Cuba after Castro; this is what I predict. And, yes, many people will stay in Cuba, but many will decide to live with relatives in Miami. It is simple, my friend—Communism does not work, and that is why the Communists operate out of fear. They are paranoid, the Communists are, because their system doesn't work, and they fear the people will revolt. That's why they need walls and mines."

"I see," said Brown.

Vega continued. "You know, I had a similar discussion with Bouchey this past week. He agreed with me that Communism does not work. He told me, 'Look at Hong Kong and compare it to mainland China; look at Miami and compare it to Havana; look at West Berlin and compare it to East Berlin back before the wall came down. That is what Bouchey told me, Brown. One works, the other doesn't."

"That's true," said Brown. "Bouchey's right 'bout that shit." Then a thought suddenly hit him. "Ya know, Vega, that Berlin wall shit is a lot like the stop-loss crap going on."

"What do you mean?"

"Well, you see, the Berlin wall was 'bout keeping East Berlin folks in East Berlin. It wasn't a wall to keep others out; it was a wall to keep people *in*. Fuckin' stop-loss shit's the same way—keep Army soldiers in the Army so they can't leave the Army. That's Communism right there, buddy."

Vega smiled. "Yes, that is very interesting, my friend. Yes, I guess the Army is like Communism." He rubbed his chin for a couple of seconds, and then he said, "I have been thinking, my friend. The U.S. has to be careful in the Middle East right now because the Middle East is a lot like Latin America."

"How's that, Vega?"

"Honor, my friend. These are honor countries, honor societies. Pride and family are big in the Middle East, just like they are big in Latin America. The U.S. has to be careful in dealing with Saddam Hussein."

"That's true," said Brown.

"Pride is big in Iraq. Trust me when I say this, Brown—Saddam Hussein gets a lot of support by being stubborn to the Big Yankee. He stands up to the United States, and people there love that."

"I see," said Brown. He was thinking at the same time, *This is cool, man—me and Vega passing time by talkin' 'bout politics and shit. Vega knows his shit because he's lived through some of this crap.*

"Standing up to the Big Yankee is popular, Brown. Right now we have a troop buildup around Iraq. The British are doing the same."

"Yeah," said Brown. "I've been following that shit on the Internet. Heck, the 1-22's headin' to Kuwait. We're going home to Texas, but they's heading to Kuwait. We lucked out, buddy."

"Roger that, my friend. God be with us. Yes, we are lucky. I hope the U.S. and British know what they are doing. Saddam Hussein is like a Communist too—I've read in magazines that he is paranoid. War with the United States will make him popular. That is what I think."

Vega slowly stood up to stretch, and then he started pacing around Tower Three. Brown, still sitting on the wooden stool, kept scanning his sector.

Shit, man, a package from my Tywanna, he thought. *I hope that package comes this morning when I get off shift. Bet anything it's that Rolex I wanted.*

"My God, my God," Vega suddenly said in a loud voice. "Some of the graffiti on this tower is sinful."

"Free speech," said Brown. He was smiling. "You know the deal, buddy."

"Yes, but the 666 graffiti is especially bad," said Vega. "At least it is followed by 'Jesus rules!'" He then approached Brown, who was still sitting on the nearby stool.

"Brown, my friend, I am not here to intrude on your privacy. I do know that you may wish to convert to Islam, and that is your business, but I would like you to read something of mine."

Ah, man, here we go, thought Brown. *Vega's the religious type, and I know he ain't too crazy 'bout me thinkin' of being Muslim. Heck, he's always readin' the Bible and stuff.*

He asked Vega, "Okay, what is it?"

Vega reached into his right BDU cargo pocket and pulled out a piece of paper. "Brown, my friend," he said, "please read this." He walked over to Brown and handed him a sheet of folded notebook paper.

Brown shifted to his left and took the paper Vega handed him. He unfolded it and read the typewritten note:

No Jesus—No Heaven; Know Jesus—Know Heaven.

The Ten Commandments Aren't Multiple Choice.

Hang out for Jesus—He Hung out for Us.

Abortion? What Part of "Thou Shall Not Kill" Don't You Understand?

Brown noticed a couple of blank lines followed by another double-spaced paragraph. He read the paragraph:

I can do all things through Christ which strengthens me. The road to success is not straight. There is a curve called Failure, a loop called Confusion, speed bumps called Friends, red lights called Enemies, and caution lights called Family. You will have flats called Jobs. But if you have a spare called Faith, and a driver called Jesus, you will make it to a place called Success.

"Good stuff, Vega," Brown said after reading the paper. "This shit's cool. Got no problem with it—no problem at all."

"Good, good, Brown," Vega said, enthused. "You see, it is Jesus, my friend. Jesus Christ is the answer; Jesus is the way."

"That's cool," Brown replied as he handed the note back to Vega. There was a pause, and then a thought hit him. *Jesus is the way? Hmm ...* Then another thought hit him.

He started unbuttoning his left breast BDU pocket. Vega, standing some five feet away, looked at him attentively.

Yeah, I feel it now, thought Brown as he pulled out a folded piece of paper from the pocket. He immediately noticed smear marks and moist spots on the paper. *Hell, it's always hot and humid here in lovely Gitmo*, he thought. *My body's sweat sure done a number on this here paper*. He handed the moist paper to Vega and said, "Read this, my man."

"Yes, yes, I will my friend," said Vega. He read the paper to himself:

Praise be to God, the Merciful, the Compassionate, the Lord of the Two Worlds, and blessing and peace upon the Prince of the Prophet, our Lord and Master, Muhammad, whom God bless and preserve with abiding and continuing peace and blessings until the Day of the Faith!

"This is Muslim, Brown," Vega said in a disappointed tone. Brown smiled and said nothing, and then Vega interjected with, "You know, my friend, the Muslims borrowed a lot from the Bible. Do you know they recognize Jesus as a prophet?"

"Roger," said Brown, still smiling. "Yeah, I think I remember readin' 'bout that some time back."

"Yes, well ... this is important, Brown. I do not have anything against Muslims, and I'm sure many Muslims are good and peaceful. But as a friend, I tell you this, Brown—Jesus is the way."

"That's cool," Brown said calmly. "That's good. I'll keep that in mind."

Vega handed the paper back to Brown just as the Saber radio sounded off.

"Attention, all towers. Attention, all towers. This is the SOG. Commence radio checks in sequence at this time."

Brown reached for the black Saber and pressed the radio's mike button. He heard Rosey say "Tower Two."

He followed with "Tower Three," and then the remaining tower guards called in their radio checks.

The radio traffic ended with, "Roger, tower guards, that's a good copy. This is the SOG. Time is oh four hundred hours. Five more hours to go, fellas. Stay alert; stay alive. SOG out."

Vega stood up and started gathering his stuff. He said, "Well, Brown, it is always a pleasure to talk to you. Papa Smurf will be around to do more tower checks later. I think he'll be here around six o'clock."

"That's cool," replied Brown as he was buttoning up his left breast BDU pocket.

Vega, now standing next to the footlocker, quickly grabbed his M16, Kevlar, and TA-50 gear. He snapped together his pistol belt and then slung his M16 over his right shoulder, placing his Kevlar atop his head. He started walking toward the tower ladder.

"Vaya con Dios, Brown. That means 'Go with God,' but I like to say 'Go with Jesus.'" He started descending the tower ladder, and then he looked back at Brown. "Always go with God, Brown; always go with Jesus."

"Roger that," replied Brown.

CHAPTER 4

Jerome Brown, the third of three children, grew up in Lubbock, Texas. His parents were Bertha and Jim Brown.

Jim Brown was a forty-year-old truck driver who got his name in honor of the famed football player many consider the greatest running back ever; Bertha, at forty-one, made her living as a cook in an elementary school.

Jamaal, now a broad-shouldered man of twenty-three, was the couple's firstborn. Since early on, Jamaal's passion had always been music, especially blues and rock and roll. When he was a young boy, Jamaal's bedroom walls were plastered with posters of his favorites: Clapton, B. B. King, Hendrix, and Buddy Guy. When he was seven, Jim and Bertha bought him his first guitar; at fourteen, Jamaal played in his first band.

Like many youngsters with a passion for music, Jamaal dreamt of making it big. "Gonna be a big star like B. B. King and Buddy Guy," he would often tell his friends. Going to college didn't appeal to Jamaal. He just wanted to play his guitar. But then, as the years ticked away, reality set in: the bands he was part of were lucky just to get small local gigs, which barely paid for gas money. Then add the fact that Jamaal was still living with his parents, who occasionally would remind him, "Can't be livin' off us forever, son," and Jamaal realized it might be time to "get a real job."

That's why, in 1999, Jamaal took a job as a prison guard at a prison in Lubbock. The steady paycheck was sufficient for him to get his own apartment and to better provide for Jenny, his girlfriend.

Today, Jamaal still chases the dream of making it big with a band—he's still playing those local gigs a couple of nights a week. And Jenny, still his steady girlfriend for some nine years now, is pregnant with their first.

***

Jim and Bertha's second child was a girl, Chantel. Now twenty-three, Chantel is wrapping up her degree from Texas Tech—she's slated to graduate in May of 2003 with a degree in business and a minor in fine arts.

Always one with a creative flair, Chantel hopes to make it in the cutthroat New York fashion industry once she graduates. She's got her game plan all figured out:

Starting salary at a recently opened design shop—thirty-four thousand before taxes

My portion of the monthly rent for a cheap Manhattan apartment, assuming I find three roommates—twelve hundred dollars

My student loan debt comes to almost three hundred per month

Tight, it'll be tight, but I'm gonna make it, she reminded herself not too long ago. *Just got done with finals. One more semester to go, and then it's hello, New York City. I'm gonna make it. I'll wait tables on the side if I have to.*

***

The last of the Brown children was Jerome. As a youngster, Jerome was okay at most things he tried out for. He was an okay Little League baseball player, an okay French horn player—overall, an okay student. He didn't have the passion for music that Jamaal had, nor the creative flair of his sister, Chantel. But Jerome was okay, and he was okay with that.

But then came the teenage years: pimples, an interest in girls, peer pressure. That's when Jerome started hangin' with the wrong crowd—the kids who boozed and did drugs and skipped school because they didn't care for school and schoolwork. Jerome wasn't a bad kid; he was an okay kid caught between the demands and pressures of school versus the demands and pressures of his friends. Besides, the only school subject Jerome cared for was history. It was the only thing that made sense to him; he didn't care for everything else.

And so it was—uninterested in all that "other school stuff"—Jerome, at the age of seventeen, did what his clique of friends did—he quit high school, moved into a studio apartment with his pals, and supported himself by working odd jobs at minimum wages. Such a lifestyle was okay for Jerome, at least at first, but as the weeks turned into months, Jerome began to realize things about his friends and, more importantly, about himself:

> *I like reading newspapers every day—my friends don't give a shit 'bout the news and politics and what's going on in the world. I can't talk to them 'bout politics and shit 'cause they just don't care. And I don't like this poverty lifestyle crap. I've got nothing against the poor, but I hate being poor. I don't mind working extra jobs to save some money. I like having my own shit, like a car. My friends, they don't mind bummin' rides, always asking for shit: 'Hey, can I borrow twenty bucks? Can I borrow your shirt? Can you buy me a beer?' My friends don't seem to be bothered by poverty. I know the poor need helpin', and I want to help 'em, but I can't help 'em if I'm poor myself.*

It was this realization—that he was different from his circle of friends—that finally led Brown to get his own apartment, his own car, and to obtain his GED. The latter he accomplished when he was eighteen.

And then came the all-important conversation he had three years ago with Bill Wright. Brown was nineteen at the time, and both he and Wright were working for a landscaping company. The conversation took place during a lunch break from a tree-trimming job.

"I'll soon have to take a couple weeks off because my AT is coming up," Wright said as he sipped Mountain Dew. He and Brown were eating cold sandwiches and sipping sodas while sitting Indian-style under the shade of a large tree they had just trimmed.

"What's AT?" asked Brown. He was working on a ham sandwich.

"Annual training. I joined the National Guard last year," Wright said. "We do a weekend drill once a month and a two-week drill once a year. That two-week drill is called AT."

"I see," said Brown, curious. "And how do you like that National Guard thing? How much does it pay, man?"

"I like it, dude. Sucks that I gotta keep my hair short, military-style, but I like the National Guard. I get about a hundred fifty bucks for the weekend drills. The two-week AT will bring me about, oh ... eight hundred bucks. Food's free during those two weeks too. But lemme tell you something, Brown."

"What's that?" He was all ears.

"Dude, the best thing about the Army National Guard is the educational benefits."

"Yeah, like what?"

"Got me the GI Bill, man. And the Texas Army National Guard has their own tuition-assistance program on top of that."

"For real?"

"Yep. Real. I'm going to vocational school at night, and my GI Bill and tuition assistance pays for the whole thing. I should be getting my masonry apprenticeship certificate in less than a year."

"Sounds good," Brown said.

"Dude, my uncle in Dallas makes serious bank in concrete. He promised me a job too—starting pay is thirteen fifty an hour plus benefits. As soon as I finish school, I'm heading to Big D to work for my uncle."

"Cool, man," Brown said. "But what about the National Guard stuff?"

"It's easy to switch units," Wright said. "I'm sure I'll find a National Guard unit around Dallas. I've got a three-year obligation."

Brown was interested. He researched the National Guard some more on his own, and in the end—especially because of the educational benefits—he decided to give it a shot.

***

After eight weeks of basic training at Fort Jackson, South Carolina, Jerome Brown, age nineteen at the time, started drilling with the Second Battalion, 142nd Infantry (Mechanized) Texas Army National Guard unit, a unit based in his hometown of Lubbock; it was the unit where co-worker Bill Wright also drilled. Brown kept his landscaping job and did his once-a-month National Guard weekend drills, and he also decided to put that GI Bill to use by enrolling in courses at a local community college. It was there that he met a beautiful beautician student named Tywanna Banks.

CHAPTER 5

As soon as Vega left Tower Three, Brown went back to scanning his tower sector.

Man, this shit's boring. Let's see ... He started thinking about his fellow Fifth Squad members of First Platoon, but then his mind shifted to his Big Four.

Should I ETS in April? Probably, man. My four years will be up. They's offering good reenlistment bonuses right now, but four years is enough. And my chances of getting stop-lossed are much smaller if I ETS now. And if I stay in the Guard, there's a chance our unit will get activated again.

Convert to Islam? Definitely heading that way 'cause Islam speaks to me. Vega's a good dude and all, and I know he's selling me hard on Christianity, but Islam speaks to me. Pray, do good, help the poor. Plus, Islam gives me a road map on how I should live my life—no drugs, no alcohol, no credit cards.

Pop the question to Tywanna? I think so. Time to hook up permanently with my T. I feel it, man—I feel good 'bout me and Tywanna together.

And the last of the Big Four: *The package. Wonder what that package is all 'bout. Bet anything T got me that Rolex. Bet that's the package, man. Just hope it comes this morning. Hey, it'll be like Christmas.*

He took a sip of warm Coke. He then started pacing around Tower Three to stretch his legs and to help him stay awake.

Got my Big Four down. What else, man? Oh yeah, I was thinkin' 'bout my fellow Fifth Squadders right before Vega came up. Whitcomb, Bouchey, got Python. Next cot's Johnston's.

He took a seat on the tower stool and started thinking about Johnston.

Johnston's a natural athlete. God, he's tall. Must be six five. And it's all muscle, man. He ain't got a bit of fat on him. I swear that dude's got black blood in him 'cause he's such a good jock. I bet he's got like a two fifty average in bowling. Saw it with my own two eyes. There we are at the Gitmo bowling alley, and I'm back there sipping on a Corona, and there's Johnston bowling strike after strike after strike. Dude's amazing, man.

He took a sip of Coke.

Shit, it was Johnston who saved my ass by bear-hugging me and getting me out of that fight with the Marine jarhead. Friggin' jarhead, man—that dude started it all by looking at me funny. Hell, if it wasn't for Johnston, a bunch of jarheads would have probably rushed me 'cause them jarheads sure are tight; they stick together and all. I remember yellin', "King Kong ain't got nothin' on me!" Good thing Johnston pulled me out of that tangle 'cause there was plenty of jarhead Marines at the Windjammer Club that night. They would've opened up a can of "whoop ass" on me if Johnston hadn't been there.

Brown scratched an itch on the right side of his nose. He kept scanning his sector.

Johnston told me he was a football stud in high school. Said he played quarterback and was recruited by some colleges, even Texas Tech. I asked him once, "Why the fuck didn't you play college ball?" And that's when Johnston told me his knees are all fucked up. "Had four knee operations, Brown." He still has the arm, though—the quarterback arm—'cause I saw Johnston tossing a football with Rosey the other day, and the dude can still throw real good.

Brown shifted on the stool to get more comfortable. He arched his back to stretch it, and he did some shoulder shrugs to loosen up.

Johnston's talented when it comes to heavy equipment and shit. I swear he's got every kind of driving license, man, CDL included. Shit, Johnston told a bunch of us Fifth Squadders he makes eighteen bucks an hour operating heavy construction equipment. Fact is there's plenty of highway construction going on 'round Lubbock. He drives a huge grader, I think, or maybe a bulldozer. Anyway, Johnston can drive anything, and he makes good money at it too.

Brown thought about all the construction work going on at Gitmo. Buildings were going up everywhere. A new medical clinic for the detainees was almost finished. *And it's Halliburton that's getting all these big contracts. Big bucks, man, big bucks earned off the backs of the poor friggin' migrant workers earning a buck or two an hour, or some puny wage shit like that. Greed right there. Corporate greed. Golden rule at play again—he who has the gold rules.*

Those poor migrant workers—they's Filipinos, Jamaicans, Pakistanis, or Indians. The Filipinos, man, they's a fun bunch, always smiling and laughing and shit. That's what I notice 'bout 'em. And you rarely see one of 'em taller than five feet six inches. Short and thin or short and chubby—that's how the Filipinos look. Brown had seen the Filipino migrant workers drinking beer in their shantytown after work. He'd noticed too that when they weren't drinking, they were either cooking meals or playing Ping-Pong.

Shit, there's one weird thing 'bout them Filipinos. Even though a lot of them have Spanish last names, they don't speak Spanish. Shit's weird. Brown recalled that the 2-142 had many guys who spoke Spanish, especially the Valley dudes in Third Platoon. When the Spanish-speaking soldiers would work the vehicle checkpoints and speak Spanish to the Filipino workers, the workers would say they didn't speak Spanish. *Shit, Vega told me just the other day he looked at a migrant worker's last name—I think it was de la Cruz—printed on the dude's shirt and asked, "How can your last name be de la Cruz and you don't speak Spanish?" The worker said, "I don't speak*

Spanish. Speak English and Tagalog." Interesting shit, if you ask me—Spanish last name and can't speak Spanish.

He took another sip of Coke from his Coke can. The Coke was now warm.

The Pakistanis and Indians, man, you'll never see them drinking booze in the shantytown. Them dudes don't drink. You rarely see the Pakistanis or Indians smile or laugh either. I can't ever tell those two apart—to me, Pakistanis and Indians look alike. They're both a serious bunch. They're all slim too, borderline thin, every single one of 'em. Brown had read that Pakistanis and Indians were enemies back in their own countries. Out here, though, they were all working hard to send their puny wages back home to their families. The Pakistanis and Indians didn't fight each other here.

Brown started doing shoulder shrugs.

One thing 'bout them Pakistanis is they's Muslim, and I once heard about a Pakistani migrant worker here who left a shank behind for a detainee. Can you imagine a poor MP dude doing his rounds and some detainee stabbing him with a shank? Thank God that shit didn't happen 'cause luckily an MP found the shank. Halliburton found out which migrant worker had left the shank behind too, and then they sent that migrant worker's ass back home.

Brown thought about the Jamaicans. They were a fun-loving bunch. They smiled all the time and laughed even louder than the Filipinos. Brown noticed they spoke English differently than Americans. *They's the only migrant workers who brought female workers with 'em. Not sure why that is—no Filipino or Indian or Pakistani women here, but we do have female Jamaican migrant workers. They work in the Sea Galley mess hall. And them Jamaicans, well, they's all tall, man—tall and big. The Jamaican women are tall too. Quite a few are pretty.*

Brown took a quick sip of Coke.

Friggin' Halliburton, man—making big profits off the backs of migrant workers. Shit ain't right. Greed. Injustice right there. Shit, Halliburton's an American company—they should be givin' all those construction jobs to Americans. Yeah, I know Americans won't work for a puny two bucks an hour, but they'll work for ten bucks an hour. It's all greed. And there's somethin' else: all the Halliburton foremen and managers here are white Anglos. It's a fact, man. I know what I see. Management's white, the migrant workers all have dark skin or yellow skin. Management's all American or Canadian or British or South African. Injustice right there too. Halliburton should let people of color have some of them top-paying foreman and management jobs.

Brown rubbed his eyes and face with his hands, and then he stood up to stretch his legs. After a few seconds, he looked at his black Timex watch. It read 4:30. *Good*, he thought. *Less than five hours to go on this boring shift.*

He sat on the stool again and resumed scanning his sector. *Whose cot's next to Johnston's? That would be Ricardo Ruas. Rosey. Shit, man, I never thought Rosey would deploy to Gitmo, 'cause that motorcycle accident he had fucked up his left leg pretty bad. He still has an ugly purple scar running down his leg.*

Brown thought about Rosey racing motorcycles. He had won trophies and everything. Brown was highly impressed. Brown thought back about their training at Fort Hood. It had been challenging. They had gone through physical training every day: squad and platoon maneuvers, riot-control training, and detainee ops. The weather had been hot and humid too, made worse while wearing QRF—Quick Reaction Force—gear.

Brown had thought Rosey wouldn't cut it because of his bad leg, but Rosey had pulled through. *He hung with us, man, unlike some of the broke dicks in our unit. Sure, I think some of our broke dicks are legit—they got legit injuries—but others are shamers, man, faking injuries and shit. Rosey ain't no broke dick.*

Brown remembered back in August when Rosey chased a guy called a Mango Rat up the hills by one of the vehicle checkpoints. The Mango Rats were from another military unit at Gitmo, and they were always testing guys in Brown's unit to make sure they were doing their jobs right. *Like photographing Camp Delta, man—that's a big no go here. If we see anyone photographing Camp Delta, we report that shit to our higher-ups right away. MPs on the ground then do their thing. Every time someone tries to photograph Camp Delta, it always ends up being one of those Mango Rat dudes trying to take a picture and testing us to make sure we's alert and doing our jobs.*

Brown had no idea how the name Mango Rat came up. *Maybe that shit has to do with all the banana rats we got here. Man, 'em banana rats look like big groundhogs or possums. They's light brown in color and got 'em deep black eyes. So many of 'em here, and they ain't afraid of people either. Shit, banana rats will get up to eight feet from ya, and then they'll scoot away.* Brown chuckled at the way he and his buddies threw pebbles at the rats to scare them off.

There's so many banana rats here on Gitmo that the government hired that hunter dude to kill 'em. Hunter dude shows up with his .22 rifle and his John Deere ATV. Shit, I remember when me, Rosey, and Johnston were working the vehicle checkpoint one night, and that hunter dude showed up. Brown recalled that the guy's name wasn't on their manifest log, so they reported it to their master sergeant who was working the commo (communications) room. The master sergeant told them the hunter could pass their checkpoint and do his thing.

"Killed about fifteen thousand banana rats so far this year," the hunter dude told us that night. "*Just too many of them. They ruin the vegetation.*" Then he said he hoped the iguanas would go off the endangered species list someday 'cause they were multiplying like the rats.

Brown stood up. He slowly stretched his back and neck, and then he cracked his knuckles.

Man, I hope I get that package this morning. Heck, if I'd known, I would've told Tywanna to wait and give me the package when I get home 'cause the mail's unpredictable here. Shit's all jacked up—mail service here is one big goat rope, one big soup sandwich. Fuck. Anyway, at least T sent it DHL. 'Cause of that, I should get the package.

He sat back down on his stool.

What the hell was I thinkin' 'bout? Oh yeah, Rosey charging that Mango Rat dude up a hill. Shit was cool, man. Mango Rat soldier was all disguised and trying to compromise our position. He tried crossing the vehicle checkpoint area by foot to sneak in close to Camp Delta. Well, Rosey saw the dude and started chasing him. Good old Rosey. Full battle rattle load, ninety-five-degree heat, and he's running after that Mango Rat. Rosey ain't no broke dick, that's for sure.

Brown knew Rosey could have stayed back at Fort Hood and gotten himself a paper-pushing job, some easy ride-the-gravy-train job. *But, nah, not Rosey. He bit the bullet and decided to deploy. He sucked it up and drove on. I gotta tip my hat to him for that.*

Brown recalled Rosey telling the Fifth Squadders he was once a good baseball player. He played catcher and apparently was good enough to play junior college ball. *But then he told us he started foolin' 'round with girls and shit, and down went his baseball playing.* Brown knew Rosey was now a mechanic at a car dealership back in Lubbock, and he knew Rosey had plans of becoming a city cop someday.

Brown suddenly stood up, and then he walked to his CamelBak that was hanging from a nail on one of the four tower support poles. He gingerly placed the CamelBak black tubing in his mouth, turned the ON/OFF valve to the ON position, and sucked in some cool water. After three gulps, he turned the valve off.

He then looked inside Camp Delta. *Ain't no escaping from that motherfuckin' Camp Delta.* He glanced down at his watch, and then he pressed the top left button to illuminate the small green screen. The time was 0448.

Suddenly, something caught his peripheral vision, something to his left. Brown immediately turned in that direction. *That's some huge moth,* he thought as he saw what had alerted him. A big white moth. Moths, attracted by the bright lights, were always flying around the fences and the spotlights.

Holy shit! Daaaaamn! In a split second, Brown witnessed an owl swooping down and catching the moth in flight. The owl landed softly on the ground some twenty feet away and started chewing away at his catch. Brown could see the moth flapping away in desperation as the owl kept chewing. *Shit, that was fast! Owl just grabbed that huge-ass moth in midair and got himself a snack.*

He started thinking: *That's power right there, man—might makes right. The moth was big, but the owl's bigger. It's just like I mentioned to Vega earlier tonight: What the fuck can Castro do? 'Course the dude hates us Yankee gringos, but what can he do? Take on Uncle Sugar? Nah, man, Uncle Sugar's that big owl, that big owl with the power. Shit, Uncle Sam can have Castro's ass for breakfast, lunch, dinner, and a midnight snack. Castro can't do shit to us.*

Brown did a set of toe raises to stretch his calves, and then he started doing shoulder shrugs.

That owl-versus-moth thing reminds me 'bout the history of this place. Brown recalled what he knew about Gitmo. *It started with Teddy Roosevelt. Uncle Sam didn't care much for Spain being in Cuba, so we fought their ass and freed Cuba. Shit, I remember it like it was yesterday when Bouchey told me 'bout TR saying, "Speak softly and carry a big stick." Uncle Sam, man—there's a big stick for ya. As far as I'm concerned, the U.S. is one big stick, one big swingin' dick, just like that big owl 'gainst the moth.*

Who can fuck with us? For real. Brown knew about power. He knew that Iraq was no match for Stormin' Norman back in the early nineties and that Hussein wouldn't be a match either if the United States decided to take him on. *I ain't pushing for war, but I know the Iraqi army can't match up to our power. It's all power, man. Owl versus moth.*

He turned around and walked back to his tower stool. He took a seat.

I dig history. TR swinging his big stick. We kick Spain out of Cuba, Puerto Rico, and the Philippines. That's what Bouchey told me in June, I think it was. Yeah, it was June 'cause we had just gotten here.

So we kick Spain's ass. Then we notice this beautiful bay here in Cuba called Guantanamo, and it sure would make a good naval station for us, so we go to the Cubans we just freed and ask them if we could rent the forty square miles of Guantanamo Bay. Bouchey told me we set the rent at twenty-five hundred dollars per year forever—in perpetuity, he told me. Some sweet-ass fuckin' deal right there.

Brown remembered Bouchey telling him that Castro tried to take his case to the World Court to end the lease but could not. A lease in perpetuity could only be broken by the two signing parties. Uncle Sam liked the Gitmo lease deal and didn't want to end it. *Power right there, man—power. He who has the gold rules. That's why powerful Uncle Sugar still pays Castro's Communist ass twenty-five hundred dollars per year to lease Gitmo. Sweet. Power. Big stick. Big swinging stick. Big swinging dick—go ahead and try fucking with me. Owl and moth right there, and we's the owl. He who has the gold rules.*

CHAPTER 6

At 0500, Brown called in his hourly radio check. He was sitting on the wooden swivel stool. *Man, four more hours to go*, he thought. *I can't wait to get off shift, head back to the hooch, and see if that package came in. Rolex, man—that's my guess.*

He grabbed his Coke can and took a quick sip from it, and then he went back to scanning his sector. *I need to keep my head in the game; otherwise, the Z-monster will get the best of me. Falling asleep is the big no go.*

All right, who else is in our squad, man? Got Whitcomb, Bouchey, pussy-chasing Python, Johnston, and Rosey—that's the whole row of cots to the right in hooch 1305. Alrighty then, row across from that—across from Rosey—it's Blackwell. Blackwell's the next Fifth Squadder.

He shifted on his stool to get more comfortable. He visually scanned his sector and started thinking about Blackwell.

Good old West Texas boy right there in Blackwell, he thought. *Old dude too. Shit, I think Blackwell's forty years old or some shit like that. I know he's the oldest dude in our squad. Got the gray hair thing going, potbelly too.* Brown knew Blackwell had been a peanut farmer who had gone bust and now worked for a peanut wholesaler. Blackwell was constantly bitching about how much of a pay cut he was taking because of the deployment to Gitmo. He knew Ralston, a fellow Fifth Squadder and a professional chef in civilian life, was also

49

taking a pay cut. Ralston didn't talk about the pay cut much, but Blackwell sure did.

Man, when I think 'bout it, we Fifth Squadders are all different. Whitcomb, he's a pretty quiet guy, but he'll sometimes talk 'bout his girlfriend and guns and cars; Bouchey talks 'bout books and politics and law; Python talks 'bout pussy and more pussy; Johnston and Rosey talk 'bout sports and bikes and girls and cars; Mini Me don't talk much—he's more of a listener; Vega talks 'bout Jesus and religion; Harrison talks 'bout sports and girls with Rosey and Johnston; Ralston, the chef, talks 'bout how the food sucks here at Gitmo; Blackwell bitches 'bout taking a pay cut and 'bout his problems with the IRS.

Brown remembered well when Blackwell told him about how he went bust as a peanut farmer. That was back in November, after they had returned from their October R & R. Brown, Blackwell, and Vega had been working the main vehicle checkpoint when Blackwell talked about going bust because of the IRS.

"How the fuck can I owe the IRS money when I didn't make money that year?" I remember Blackwell saying. He also said something like, "Damn IRS. That's one government outfit that don't know jack shit 'bout equipment upgrades and capital expenditures. They ain't farmers, and they don't know shit 'bout farming."

Brown remembered Blackwell saying that he still owed the IRS back taxes. Brown figured that his IRS shit stressed him out, especially since he had a wife and four kids to support.

Brown took a sip of warm Coke and thought more about Blackwell. *He's a direct dude—very direct—like a lot of West Texans. Hell, if he don't like something, he'll say so up front. Brown remembered the time when he was working a vehicle checkpoint with Rosey and Blackwell. A Humvee came to their checkpoint. Inside the Humvee were two female soldiers, probably from the National Guard unit out of Mississippi. One of the female soldiers was white; the other was black. After we let the Humvee pass through, Blackwell turned to me and said,*

'*That white soldier girl sure is ugly. God she's ugly.*' Direct, man—Blackwell's one direct dude.

Another thing Brown remembered about Blackwell was that he didn't care much for the hard charger. Brown wouldn't be surprised if Blackwell had written that "Kill the hard charger" graffiti. Blackwell's attitude on the hard charger went back to when the unit's deployment was brewing back in April. Rumors were circulating everywhere at their Lubbock National Guard Center. The men had heard they were deploying to Egypt; then they heard they were going to Colorado; then they heard Fort Bliss, Texas; then they heard Cuba.

Those were 'em rumors floating 'round everywhere when we got called up. 'Course that last one was true—we ended up here at Gitmo. That one 'bout Fort Bliss was also true 'cause we've got some 2-142 soldiers at Bliss right now, but word is their mission is soon coming to an end. Anyway, the story is that the hard charger told Blackwell back in April that we were headin' to Fort Carson, Colorado.

Not too long ago, Blackwell told me that Boswell's a liar pure and simple. He also told me there's a big fucking difference between cool, dry Colorado and hot and humid Gitmo, and that if we were stationed in Colorado, at least he'd get to see his family more often.

Brown looked at the dark sky. *Half-moon tonight. When it's a full moon, I can see the ocean, but not tonight. It's still dark out right now.*

He then shifted to the right a bit and looked at the well-lit Camp America compound about a quarter of a mile away. He started thinking about Blackwell again.

I know Blackwell's got bad feet 'cause 'bout a month ago, he got himself a foot profile, and ever since then, he's been working in the supply section. Blackwell's a hard worker, man, and I know he puts in a good day's work in supply. Shit, I know some dudes look down at Blackwell 'cause he's on profile and shit—'cause he's a broke dick—but most dudes know he's a hard worker. Same with Ralston, man. He too is on foot profile, but most dudes know Ralston ain't no slacker; he ain't shamin' and lookin' to get out of work.

Brown thought about the three soldiers working in the maintenance shop. The guys pulling tower guard duty and working vehicle checkpoints didn't care for the three maintenance shop soldiers because they worked easy hours: eight hours a day with Sundays off. *Our work schedule is twice as many hours, and we don't work inside the shade with fans blowing and shit. Nah, man, we's out on towers or out baking in the hot sun working checkpoints. Those damn maintenance dudes. They change a Humvee tire or change the oil. Whatever, man. Big deal. It's cake, man. Their job's a cakewalk. They ridin' a fuckin' gravy train.*

Standing and stretching his legs, Brown started pacing around the plywood floor of Tower Three. *Blackwell and Ralston ain't the only two broke dicks 'round here. I hear Second Platoon's got plenty of 'em too.*

Brown thought about the fact that before the higher-ups put stools in the towers, all the soldiers were having foot problems. Bringing stools to the towers was one rare example of higher-ups connecting with the soldiers who actually did the work. The stools prevented foot profiles and more broke dicks.

Brown returned to the tower stool and sat on it; he then resumed staring to the southwest to scan his sector.

Thinkin' 'bout this profile and broke dick shit reminds me of Molina, man. First Sergeant Molina. Dude's high-speed. All tabbed out and shit with his Ranger tab and Special Forces tab and drill sergeant patch, and all that airborne, air assault, expert infantry badge high-speed grunt-infantry stuff. Dude's a helluva soldier—lots of "been there and done that" with him 'cause he's been everywhere, man: Germany, Korea, Panama, Persian Gulf War, and shit.

Molina had been the first sergeant of the 1-142, so when that unit combined with the 2-142, he became Brown's first sergeant. Molina was always saying "mighty fine" this and "mighty fine" that. The First Squadders called him "Mighty Fine" Molina.

Molina, he don't cut slack to any broke dick—no way, Jose. I remember the time he gave us 2-142 soldiers a little pep talk when we was training back at Hood. It was right after PT, and Molina still had us in formation. That's when he said there was too many broke dicks in our unit, that some of us soldiers had to be shaming and faking injuries. I remember Molina telling us, "Men, sometimes you just gotta reach down, grab your fuckin' balls, and thank God you still have a pair. Gotta have some suck it up and drive on, men." It was beautiful; good pep talk right there.

Brown took another sip of warm Coke.

What Molina told us back then at Fort Hood was true—we did have some broke dicks in our unit who were shaming and dragging their ass. My take on it is that injuries usually start out legit, but then the broke dick soldier just keeps riding his profile so he don't have to train and work and shit. Yeah, that's what I think 'cause ... He stopped thinking because he heard *cling clang cling.*

Hmm ... Who's coming up my tower ladder?

Brown got up and walked to the tower entrance, the part where the metal ladder's edge met the tower plywood floor. He peered down.

"That you, boss?"

"Roger that, Brown," answered Sergeant First Class "Papa Smurf" Rivera. Rivera strained a bit as he climbed the tower ladder. "Your old platoon leader here. Platoon leaders are supposed to be lieutenants, but we're so short on officers they had to make an old fart like me platoon leader."

Brown extended his right hand to help hoist Rivera up unto the plywood floor. "Let me help you up, boss."

"Ah, appreciate that, mi amigo," said Rivera as he was catching his breath.

"I see you got your full battle rattle on."

"Roger that, amigo," said the fifty-three-year-old Rivera. He took a few deep breaths and started removing his TA-50 gear.

Brown took a seat on the tower stool and looked at Rivera. *Man, Papa Smurf's got more gray hair now than when we started here in June. I guess a job like platoon leader can do that shit to someone. And Papa Smurf's gotta be—what?—at least fifty. I know he was in Vietnam, so he ain't no spring chicken.*

"Well, amigo," said Rivera as he unslung his black nylon M16 sling from his right shoulder. "I'm just here doing my rounds. You good on radio batteries ... water? Need to use the head?"

"Good to go, boss," Brown responded. He noticed Rivera heading toward the big green plastic footlocker in the middle of the tower floor. "I'll probably have to drain the main vein sometime later this morning, but for now I'm good to go."

"Roger, Brown," said Rivera as he took a seat on the footlocker.

Brown noticed that Rivera was wearing those ugly brown Army-issued eyeglasses—BCGs, or birth control glasses, as they were called. *Soldier wearing those ugly-ass glasses won't ever get laid, man.*

"Well, Brown, our last shift -- we did it," Rivera said in an optimistic tone. He started removing an Army-issued brown handkerchief from his right front pant pocket.

"Roger that, boss," responded Brown. "Couple more hours of this shit, then it's pack up and fly to Fort Hood."

"That's right, Brown. We'll be at Fort Hood tonight," Rivera said. He wiped sweat off his forehead with the brown Army handkerchief. "It's been a long six months here, and Gitmo ain't no paradise, but things haven't been all that bad here."

"Shit, boss—not all that bad?" Brown said in bewilderment. "This deployment sucks big-time. Sucks *mucho grande.*"

Rivera slowly placed the handkerchief back in his right front pocket. He then replied, "Well, Brown, the weather's nice here, plus the mission ain't too tough. And we have nice things like the bowling alley, McDonald's, and Subway."

He went on to compliment the free movies at the lyceum, the cold beer at the bowling alley, the Windjammer Club and its nice pool tables, and the Tiki Bar. He thought the library had a great selection of books. "Oh, I almost forgot—the swimming pool and the gym are top-notch, and Windmill Beach is outstanding. Hell, I got my scuba diving certification there."

Brown said nothing. He kept facing Rivera.

"Brown, my friend, this Gitmo thing ain't all that bad. Compared to fuckin' Nam, this tour is paradise—I can tell you that much."

"I get what you're saying, boss," said Brown. Deciding to shift gears, he said, "Boss, tell me 'bout Nam, man. What was it like?"

"Oh, Brown, I don't care to talk about that crap."

"C'mon, boss. It's our last shift." He looked directly at Rivera. "Me and you both know we need to kill some time here. Tell me 'bout Nam, boss."

Reluctantly, Rivera said, "Well, all right, mi amigo. Anything to kill time, I guess."

"Cool," said Brown.

"I came to this country from Mexico," Rivera said. "I was young and full of cum and wet behind the ears. I could barely speak English. Anyway, I got drafted, and the next thing I knew, I was in the Rumble in the Jungle called Vietnam."

"See, boss, that's the damn shit right there," Brown said passionately. "People of color, boss—people of color like you and me—always get the shaft, man. I ain't got nothin' 'gainst white folk, but people of color always get the shaft. Ever hear of this New York politician named Charles Rangel?"

"Um ... no, can't say I know him, Brown."

"Well, Rangel thinks we should do the draft again."

Rivera extended his legs to stretch them. "Draft fucked me up, amigo. Not sure if doing another draft is a good idea."

"Yeah, but here's the catch, boss: Rangel thinks everybody should serve, including rich white boys. President Bush and Clinton—shit, everything I read says they dodged the draft. Blacks and Hispanics are the ones fighting Uncle Sam's wars."

"Well, Brown, I was there, son," Rivera said. "I served in Nam, my friend. Plenty of white guys were serving there too."

"Yeah, that might be so, boss, but I bet you them white boys were poor. They weren't the rich college type."

Rivera said nothing. He looked down at the plywood floor, and then he said, "Well, Vietnam wasn't all bad, I guess. I met some good guys in Nam. And I gotta tell you, Brown, the weed and chicks were always around. That shit kept us going. There was always plenty of dope and pussy in Vietnam. Even some of our officers partied with us."

Brown smiled and replied, "Ain't much in the chick department here, boss. Python sure tries, but based on the numbers here, there's just so few chicks."

"That's true, that's true, mi amigo. By the way, how's Python doing? Any word on that DUI of his?"

"All I know is he's got a JAG lawyer working his case. I think he's negotiating some deal instead of a court-martial. Word is he won't be on that chartered bird with us today."

"Right. That's the story I'm hearing too," said Rivera.

A few quiet seconds passed. Brown wanted Rivera to resume talking about Vietnam, so he thought of something to say to get the conversation going in that direction again.

"Ya know, boss, we should be drawing combat pay here at Gitmo. I mean the Cuban fence line is right on our tail, and Bouchey told me he read some newspaper articles saying Castro's willing to help Al-Qaeda. I know this ain't Vietnam, boss, but this Gitmo shit's real, man."

Rivera pulled out his handkerchief again. He said, "We are getting hazardous duty pay here, and that's fair enough. Combat, Brown, combat is like that Rumble in the Jungle, where I was thirty years ago. That shit was real."

"How so, boss?" asked Brown.

Rivera removed his eyeglasses and wiped the lenses with his handkerchief. "Well, my friend, I remember once we were near the Ho Chi Minh Trail. We set up this ambush—mines and all. Then we waited and waited. That's one thing few people will tell you, Brown."

"What's that?"

Rivera slowly put on his glasses, and then he said, "Combat is fucking boring most of the time, Brown, because there's a shitload of hurry up and wait in combat—hurry up to do this, to do that, then wait forever. Anyway, we waited and waited; I think we waited five hours on this ambush site. And no chicks or weed during that time, my friend. That's another thing a lot of people don't know."

"What's that, boss?"

"The chicks and smoking pot—we didn't do that shit when we were in the bush. Maybe it was an unwritten rule, but we all followed it: no smoking dope when in the bush because the enemy can smell that shit from far away. And chicks really weren't around either. Anyway, Brown, we waited maybe five hours on that ambush point. Five hours is a long time to wait, amigo. Then, all of a sudden, we saw them: the Vietcong, black pajamas and all. There was a small group of them coming down the trail. That's actually rare, my friend, seeing the Vietcong on the trail; we were expecting the North Vietnamese soldiers. We were well hidden, of course, and when the bad guys were next to the mines we had set up, well, we lit them up. Fucking bullets flying everywhere. I was scared, Brown, but we took them out. Everything was happening so fast."

"*Cool*," thought Brown. "I'm sure it's scary shit, but, hey, cool takin' the fuckers out."

Rivera folded his handkerchief and placed it back in his right front pocket. He then said, "I remember the first time I was in combat in Vietnam. We were in the bush, and the first thing our first sergeant did was take a squad of us to the perimeter to show us a dead Vietcong. I still remember what he told us. He said, 'See this dead fellow, men? This here dead Commie is the enemy. Name is Vietcong. This here little fucker tried to break through our perimeter last night. Make no mistake about it, men—these little shits are tough, and they'll fight to the end. These little pajama-wearing fucks have fought them all—the Chinese, the Japanese, the French, and now us. This fellow will try to kill you, so be on the lookout.' That's what our first sergeant told us."

"That's some tough shit, boss."

"Yep, you bet it was. I was scared too. That's what combat does sometimes—it scares you. You know, that same first sergeant told us we'd see a lot of shit in the bush, and because of that, some of us would feel like crying. He also said many of us would pee in our pants the first time we experienced bullets flying." Rivera paused for a couple of seconds, and then he said, "First Sergeant told us it was okay to cry. It was okay to pee in our pants."

"For real, boss? The first sergeant said it was okay to cry and to pee in your pants?"

"Yep, sure did. True story, mi amigo."

A few quiet seconds passed. Rivera looked down at the plywood floor. Brown looked at him and noticed he was shaking his head.

"You know, Brown, there's something else you don't hear too often about the Vietnam War."

"Oh, what's that?"

"This whole thing about war protests and spitting on American GIs and shit."

"Oh, I've heard 'bout that, boss. Read it in one of my sociology classes. College students dodging the draft, protesting the war—even soldiers coming back from Nam got involved in the antiwar movement and shit. Heard all 'bout it, boss."

"No, no, see, that's the thing people don't know," said Rivera with a tinge of frustration in his voice. "The opposite, my friend, was true too. Fact is, Brown, lots of folks were for the war. I tell you, when I returned to Texas after the war, strangers knew I was a Vietnam vet, and what did they want? They wanted to shake my hand, buy me coffee; they gave me the thumbs-up when they saw me, stuff like that. Local barber even gave me free haircuts for, like, six months. You don't hear about that stuff, my friend."

"For real, boss? Folks liked you and gave you freebies all because you were a war vet?"

"Roger that, Brown. Those folks were in favor of the war. Might have been different in the big cities like Boston, New York, and San Francisco, but in the heartland and in Texas—hell, I felt good about being a war veteran."

Brown said nothing for close to ten seconds. He pondered what Rivera had just told him. "Boss, I know this shit ain't nothing compared to Vietnam, but shit's real here too, man. We've had two suicide attempts here."

"Yes, you're right about that," replied Rivera. He was looking directly at Brown. "Actually, it's one suicide, one suicide attempt, and one combat flashback."

"Roger, boss. That poor MP's unit held a funeral for him about a month ago."

"That's right, Brown. They sure did."

Brown crossed his arms over his chest while he remained seated on the stool. He said, "Ya know, boss, the MP's unit is still divided 'bout that whole drowning thing. Some MPs claim it was a swimming accident, but others say it was a suicide. Me, I think it was a suicide."

"Me too," Rivera said.

"Shit, many of his fellow MPs told me the dude was having marital problems. He took off his clothes 'round midnight and jumped off the cliff. C'mon, man. Dude coulda went to Windmill Beach if he had wanted to go swimming."

"I'm tracking, mi amigo," said Rivera. "I'm thinking the same thing."

Brown spun his swivel stool 180 degrees and looked out a quarter mile or so toward the southwest. He zeroed in on the area next to the Sea Galley mess hall, an area partially lit from the spotlights of Camp America. He saw what he was looking for.

"There's the cross, boss—out there, right on the edge of the coast." Brown pointed to a tall white wooden cross the MP unit had erected in memory of the MP who drowned. The cross had been placed at the spot where the MP's clothes were found.

"Yes, Brown, I know the cross well," said Rivera. "I'm Catholic. I do a sign of the cross every time I see that cross."

Brown pressed on. "And poor Adams, man. That was a close call, boss. Another suicide attempt right there." He spun his stool back to face his platoon leader.

"Yes, that's true, Brown. What platoon is Adams in again?"

"Second Platoon," said Brown. "And that one involved marital problems too. Story I heard was Adams was having problems with his wife. Some guys from Second Platoon told me they found a "tell my wife I love her letter" on his cot. Everyone started running 'round looking for him. Next thing we know, Stetson and Carpenter find Adams sitting on that rock next to our supply CONEX. Adams had a loaded M16 within arm's reach, and he's chain-smoking like crazy and crying like a baby. Stetson apparently had to wrestle Adams to the ground while Carpenter got hold of the loaded M16."

"Yes, Adams was a close call too," Rivera said. "But he's doing a lot better now. Spending a few days in the navy hospital did him good, and even if we don't let him carry an M16, he's still a productive worker over at supply."

"Yeah, that's true," said Brown. "Still was a close call, though."

A few quiet seconds passed, and then Brown asked, "Boss, do ya think that whole Adams thing was 'bout some Jody shit? Somebody foolin' 'round with Adams's wife?"

"Who knows, mi amigo? Who knows?"

Brown interlaced his fingers and cracked his knuckles. He then spun his stool around, grabbed his Coke can, and took a sip. "And another close call with Diaz, boss. That one was just last week."

"Yep, another close call. Diaz is in Third Platoon, right?"

"Roger, boss."

"Poor old Diaz," Rivera said, shaking his head. "A flashback from his Vietnam days is what Diaz went through. I'm glad I don't have flashbacks from Nam. I had nightmares about it when I first got back stateside, but I haven't had a nightmare about Vietnam in ... oh ... heck, probably twenty-five years."

"That's cool," said Brown.

"Yes, it is," replied Rivera. "But you know, that's another thing lots of folks will never know."

"What's that, boss?"

"More than one Vietnam tour. You see, Brown, many of us Vietnam vets—even the guys who got drafted like me—did more than one tour in Vietnam, even though one was all we had to do."

"For real?"

"Yes, my friend. Lots of us soldiers complained and shit, but many of us volunteered to do more than one tour in Vietnam. And I mean volunteer, Brown. Nobody put a gun to our heads when it came time to re-up. The fact was, many of us liked the excitement about the whole thing. Sure, there's a lot of hurry-up-and-wait crap during combat, but there's excitement too—scary, but exciting. And like I told you earlier, there was plenty of pussy and weed in Nam. That shit was fun too."

"I'm tracking, boss," Brown said with interest. "The story I heard 'bout Diaz was he had tower guard last week during the day shift. Apparently, the hot and humid weather got him thinkin' 'bout Nam and shit. MP working Camp Delta told me he saw Diaz taking off his BDU top, and the next thing he saw was Diaz pointing his M16 inside Camp Delta and screaming, 'They're coming! They're coming! Kooks are coming!' MPs finally calmed down old Diaz. They took his weapon and brought him to the hospital."

"That's basically the same story I heard," Rivera said. "And like Adams, Diaz also recovered well. Rest did him good. He's also working supply, which is an easy job."

"Roger, boss."

Rivera rubbed his forehead and looked down at the plywood floor. "I'm a lucky man, Brown. I've got a good wife, and I've got two nice kids. And just two months ago, I found out I'm a grandpa. I can't wait to see my first grandchild, Brown."

"That's cool, man," replied Brown. "I've got nice plans of my own, boss. My ETS is in April, and I plan to get out of the Army then, marry my girlfriend, and start taking more college courses."

Rivera looked at Brown and said, "Sounds like a winner, my friend. Just make sure you marry the right girl. A good woman is not easy to find, you know, especially in this day and age, when—"

"Attention, all towers, attention, all towers." It was Staff Sergeant Harrison's voice over the radio. "This is the SOG. Commence radio checks in sequence at this time."

Brown stood up and called in his radio check. He looked at his watch. It read 5:58. *Three more hours to go*, he thought. *Can't wait to get out of here … Boy, I hope I get that package this morning.*

Rivera suddenly stood up. He started walking around the tower. "Sunrises sure are nice here at Gitmo, ain't they, Brown?"

"Sure are, boss," said Brown. He took a seat on his stool.

Rivera pointed. "That beautiful orange sun will soon pop up from the ocean."

"Yeah, I see it, boss. It's like a nice bright orange ball rising from the water."

Rivera sat down again on the large plastic footlocker. He looked down at the floor.

"Worst thing I ever saw in Nam, Brown, was one time when we were out on patrol. You know we fought with the South Vietnamese against the Communist North. I know the South eventually lost, but some of those South Vietnamese soldiers were great fighters. Their officers and leadership sucked, though, because many of those higher-ups were big-time corrupt."

"Hey, it's all corrupt at the top," Brown said, smiling. "Leadership is one big goat rope, one big soup sandwich."

"Yes, that might be," responded Rivera. "But the South Vietnamese soldiers were tough, my friend. Anyway, one time we were out on patrol, right, and these South Vietnamese soldiers who were with us caught this little boy. This boy was maybe ten years old, Brown, and the South Vietnamese soldiers suspected the boy was Vietcong, so they wanted information from him. This little boy wouldn't talk, though."

"Why's that?" asked Brown.

"Beats me," said Rivera. "Maybe the boy knew nothing, or maybe he was helping the enemy. Anyway, the South Vietnamese soldiers got tired of no answers from this boy, and that's when they placed a plastic bag over his head. They beat him, Brown, they beat this little boy. It was ugly. The South Vietnamese didn't fuck around. We American soldiers were on the sidelines with that shit—we didn't do the beating, but we watched. At one point, we had a staff sergeant tell the South Vietnamese to stop beating the poor kid and to let him breathe, but they ignored all that. To this day, Brown, I'm not sure if that boy survived—because I couldn't look at it no more, and I just turned around."

"That's some pretty tough shit, boss."

"Sure is, my friend. Combat sucks, seeing shit like that."

Rivera slowly stood up. He peered inside Camp Delta. Brown, looking toward the southeast, was observing the semicircle orange sun making its way above the ocean.

"Brown, I see the truck bringing us chow." Rivera pointed to the main gate, where the pickup truck was about to pass through. "Why don't you eat breakfast and bring me a to-go plate. I'll do your seven o'clock radio check if need be."

"Sure thing," said Brown as he stood up and put on his TA-50 gear. He then slung his M16 over his right shoulder and proceeded to descend the Tower Three ladder. In no time, he was walking toward the Quick Reaction Force trailer used to house soldiers on tower guard duty. He wanted to get a fresh Coke, and the only Coke machine was in the QRF trailer.

He kept walking toward the trailer, which was maybe a football field length away. He was walking on small crushed rocks, and that slowed him down some because his balance was a bit off, especially since he had the weight of all his gear and weapon. *Man, I hope I get that package this morning*, he thought yet again. *I bet Tywanna got me that Rolex.*

After a few minutes of walking, Brown noticed two MPs and a detainee riding in a John Deere four-wheel ATV inside Camp Delta. The MPs were transporting the detainee to the small medical clinic within the compound. One MP served as the driver, while the other MP sat adjacent to the detainee in the backseat. Brown guessed the detainee was in his forties. He noticed the detainee was missing his lower right leg.

Another amputee, he thought as he kept walking toward the QRF trailer. His mind focused on how the United States had helped Muslim fighters in Afghanistan defeat the Russians. *Mujahedin is what they's was called. Some of those former mujahedin we helped later got into the Taliban and Al-Qaeda. Man, talk 'bout full circle. One man's freedom fighter really might be another dude's terrorist, but having one man's freedom fighter twenty years later become that same man's terrorist? Shit's twisted, man.*

He kept walking toward the QRF trailer. Eventually, he passed both Tower One and Tower Two. He also noticed the bright orange sun creeping up over the ocean. *Man, they've got beautiful sunrises here at Gitmo.* He kept walking, and then his thoughts shifted back to the detainee he had just seen.

Bouchey told me the Russians left a ton of mines in Afghanistan. I figure some of these detainees here lost limbs 'cause of all them Russian mines.

A few minutes later, Brown entered the QRF trailer through the front entrance. As he entered, he noticed lots of soldiers walking around the hallway.

I recognize some of these guys. Those are soldiers from our Third Platoon cleaning this place up, but some of these soldiers I've never seen before.

He started walking down the wide hallway. The second room to the left was one of two latrines, and Brown went there to relieve himself. Afterward, he walked down the hallway some more until he came upon the fifth room on the right, the room that housed the small kitchen area.

"Mornin', Brown," came a voice behind him. Brown, who was pulling two Coke cans out of the Coke machine, quickly looked behind him. It was Ralston, holding a mop.

"Mornin', Ralston," said Brown as he placed one of the Coke cans in his right pant cargo pocket. "I guess you're part of the cleanup crew, heh?"

"Roger that," the tall Ralston replied. "Less than three hours to go, squad buddy. We're cleaning up this place pretty good."

"That's cool, man," said Brown. Then he asked, "Hey, Ralston, who are the soldiers here? I've never seen them dudes."

"Oh, those soldiers are from the Virginia National Guard. And some of them keep dragging mud on my newly mopped floors. It's hard keeping a place like this clean because—"

"Morning, fellas," said Johnston, chiming in as he entered the room. "I'm like you, Brown—I need my Coke kick in the morning." Johnston placed three quarters in the Coke machine. "And, Ralston, buddy, you're looking good in those Japanese jump boots. Still got that broke dick foot profile, I see."

"Very funny," said Ralston. "And yes, I do have a foot profile. Doc told me the best thing for my feet is tennis shoes, and that's what I'm wearing—not Japanese jump boots, thank you very much."

"Roger that," Johnston said, smiling. He grabbed his Coke can and started heading out the kitchen. Brown tagged along with him.

"Can you believe it, Brown?" Johnston said as the two Fifth Squadders exited the QRF trailer. "Our last tower shift, bro. Six months in this joint is long enough."

"Got that right," said Brown as the two walked past the large water buffalo tank holding ample amounts of potable water. "Six months is plenty long. And thank God we ain't getting stop-lossed or sent out to Kuwait or Saudi. Might be another fight in the Middle East sandbox soon."

"Yeah, you're right about that, Brown. Time to go home, man. Christmas is just around the corner. We sure are lucky to be home for the holidays."

The two kept walking toward the Army mess tent located in the southwestern portion of Camp Delta. The plain but large dark green tent served as a small mess hall to feed soldiers on tower guard duty.

In less than five minutes, Brown and Johnston reached the tent, and once there, they immediately saw that a long line of soldiers had already formed up. Johnston, who stood well above six feet, saw Rosey and Harrison toward the middle of that long line. He made eye contact with Rosey and signaled for Rosey and Harrison to join him and Brown for chow. Rosey and Harrison did just that. They gave up their spots and joined Johnston and Brown at the back of the line.

"What up, fellas?" Harrison said to Johnston and Brown as the foursome met. "Fine fucking shift. Get us some grub, do a few radio checks, then we're outta here."

"Got that right, big SOG," Johnston said. Brown nodded in approval. Rosey and Johnston high-fived each other.

The breakfast line steadily crept forward, and at one point, Harrison asked, "Hey, fellas, all your towers covered, right? Somebody manning your towers?"

"Roger," said Johnston. "Nichols from Second Platoon's got mine."

Rosey said, "Hernandez got me covered, Sarge."

Brown said, "Papa Smurf's got my tower. Remind me, y'all, to get him a to-go plate."

In line, Brown glanced at Harrison and thought more about him. *Harrison's been good to me, man. Mentor, really. I think Rivera had something to do with that. Shit all goes back to when I got into a fight with that jarhead. I was in Third Squad back then, even though I hung out with Fifth Squadders like Bouchey and Johnston and Rosey and Harrison. Then, after I got into that fight, I think Rivera pulled some strings and got me a cot in hooch 1305. Shit was cool with me, especially since I didn't care much for Third Squad. Shit, man, as soon as I moved to Fifth Squad, Harrison started talking to me and shit and giving me tips like "Don't drink too much," "Don't pick fights, bro," "Do your job and keep your nose clean, and people will respect you." Shit like that. Worked too. The dudes in Fifth Squad got along with me and all.*

What else 'bout Harrison, our squad leader? Brown concentrated. In his opinion, Harrison's military uniform sure did look fine. Whitcomb's BDUs were neatly pressed and starched, and his black boots were always spit-shined—even in dusty Gitmo. *But Harrison's are even better—his BDUs are even more starched, and his boots are even shinier than Whitcomb's.*

Brown watched Harrison closely. He guessed Harrison to be about five feet nine and 190 pounds. *That's all muscle too—rock-solid pecs, big biceps, small waist, thighs like tree trunks. Harrison was a high school football star, man. Running back. Ran with those big thighs. Carried the ball. He told me he was just so-so in college, though. Dropped out due to injuries. I think he coaches his son's team now. That's cool.* Brown knew Harrison to be a good all-around athlete. A jock of all trades. *Basketball, volleyball, weight lifting, running ... everything, man. Harrison's not a bowler like Johnston, and I know he can't swim, but the dude's coordinated.*

***

Ten minutes later, the four Fifth Squadders were ordering breakfast from the serving line. Brown, unsure what Rivera wanted for chow, played it safe and ordered the works for his platoon leader: scrambled eggs, sausage, bacon, biscuits and gravy, pancakes, and home fries. He told the last cook in the serving line, "Wrap this plate up with plastic wrap, would you, please? I don't want flies all over Papa Smurf's breakfast."

The four Fifth Squadders balanced their breakfast items on paper plates and exited the mess tent. Some thirty meters away was an old wooden picnic table situated under a large tree. The four men sat at the picnic table. Other soldiers, unknown to them, were already there eating.

Just a couple of minutes after sitting down, Brown noticed a group of soldiers raising the American flag up a white metal pole not too far from the picnic table. Then, over a loudspeaker, came the start of the national anthem.

"Group, attention! Present—arms!" yelled Harrison as soon as he heard the start of the anthem. Every soldier immediately stood up and rendered a salute, a salute that lasted throughout the anthem. When the playing of the anthem ended, Harrison said, "Order—arms!" and that's when every soldier ended his salute, took his seat, and resumed eating.

"About fucking time we have our anthem playing here."

Brown looked to his right. The soldier who had just spoken those words had his BDU arm sleeves rolled up. Brown noticed a tattoo on the soldier's left forearm, a tattoo that read NASCAR RULES.

"Damn detainees get all this religious call-to-prayer music over loudspeakers," said the same soldier. "Only fair we should get to hear our anthem play."

A few soldiers at the picnic table nodded in approval. One soldier chimed in with, "Amen to that."

Brown thought, *Nothing wrong with the playing of our anthem. Shit, I'm surprised it hasn't been played sooner. This anthem playing started just ... what? Oh, maybe two weeks ago.*

Five minutes later, Brown, who was a quick eater, was done with his breakfast. He got up and threw his paper plate, white plastic utensils, and his empty Coke can in the large metal wastebasket near the tree they were under. He started heading toward Tower Three, all while balancing Rivera's to-go plate with his left hand. Rosey and Johnston were just behind him; Harrison, still eating at the picnic table, was talking to soldiers Brown did not recognize.

Can't wait to arrive at Fort Hood tonight, thought Brown as he walked on the crushed gray rocks leading to his tower.

As to my Big Four, well .... ETS in April? Yeah, man, that's the thing to do. Convert to Islam? A go on that one too. Islam speaks to me. Pop the question to Tywanna? Definitely leaning toward yes on that one too. I love her. I love her and Danielle. And then he thought, *The package—wonder what the package's all 'bout. Boy, I hope it's coming this morning.*

Brown's thoughts drifted back to October and his ten-day leave. All the 2-142 soldiers were given ten days of earned leave.

Y'all can burn your ten days by spending your vacation here at Gitmo, Brown remembered Rivera telling them. *Or y'all can fly back home and visit your loved ones. I don't know about y'all, but I sure miss my family. I know that's where I'm heading.* Flying to the States and back was what most of the men did, despite the fact that travel time ate up two of their days.

Not everyone could leave at once; so Brown, Bouchey, Rosey, and Vega had taken their vacation time in early October, while Harrison, Mini Me, and Ralston had taken theirs in late October. Python, Whitcomb, and Johnston had decided to stay put in sunny Gitmo. Blackwell, often bitching about money and his need to have more of it, had opted to keep working and to cash in his leave when the unit deactivated in late December at Fort Hood.

A day of travel to Texas, eight fun-filled days with Tywanna and precious little Danielle, and a day to return to Gitmo was how Brown had spent his military leave. And it had been during that leave time—on day four—that Brown, Tywanna, and Danielle had spent some time at the Amarillo mall, the mall where a certain used Rolex watch caught Brown's eye—a Rolex he wanted but couldn't afford, a Rolex that a couple of months later, he was convinced constituted the package Tywanna said she sent him.

***

"Hey, amigo, thanks for the breakfast chow." Rivera extended his hands to take the to-go plate from Brown. "That's pretty impressive, Brown—climbing a tower ladder with your full battle rattle while carrying a breakfast plate."

"Ah, boss, ain't nothing but a thing," said Brown as he stepped onto the tower's plywood floor.

"Well, I appreciate this, my friend. I'm pretty hungry this morning."

Brown proceeded to remove his TA-50 gear and place it in the corner next to the stool. He then unslung his M16 and placed it next to his TA-50 gear.

"Wasn't sure what to get you, boss, so I got you the works." He took a seat on the tower swivel stool.

"Works for me," said Rivera as he removed the plastic wrapping from the breakfast plate.

"Sorry I didn't bring you a drink, but I wasn't sure if you're a juice guy or a chocolate milk guy. I got a Coke can in one of my cargo pockets—do you want it?"

"Nah, mi amigo," said Rivera as he took a seat on the large footlocker. "Don't worry about it. The water in my CamelBak will do just fine." He started eating.

Brown removed his Coke can from his right cargo pocket, and then he spun the stool and looked inside Camp Delta. The detainees had already started exercising. Brown watched some detainees stretching and jogging in place. He saw detainees doing calisthenics, and some were taking showers too. The entire exercise and shower area was fenced off, and the showers were private. He noticed a couple of detainees practicing martial arts moves.

Overall, I think the detainees are a pretty disciplined force, he thought. *Many detainees practice martial arts. I think they're disciplined fighters who take their shit seriously.*

He spun his stool around and started visually scanning his sector. "Tell you what, boss," Brown said. "Some things were okay about this place, but we definitely had our speed bumps here." He was staring at the blue ocean, now clearly visible. "Take promotions, for example. Yeah, some guys deserved to get promoted, but other guys didn't. Some dudes got promoted even when they didn't want to, man."

"That's true, my friend," said Rivera as he scooped up some of his scrambled eggs with a plastic fork.

Brown then thought about the time Lopez from Third Platoon was out on patrol and claimed he had lost his night vision goggles. "You remember the case of the lost nods? Gosh, boss, that sure was jacked up."

"Yep, roger that, Brown," responded Rivera, even though his mouth was filled with scrambled eggs.

"He changes his tune once he finds out he might be charged to pay for the loss. Shit's jacked up, boss."

"Yes, you're right about that," Rivera said. He swallowed hard, and then he took a few sips of water from his CamelBak strapped to his back.

"Damn Captain Boswell, boss—I can't say otherwise. Boswell orders two shakedown inspections, and not only for our unit but for all service members in Camp America." A shakedown inspection meant that all personnel had to stay within Camp America. No one could leave. "Friggin' Lopez first said his nods were lost," Brown continued. "And then he said they were stolen, and Boswell has the balls to believe him. Boss, do you remember how pissed off those other units were at us? They was mad as hell at us for them two shakedown inspections. I don't blame them for being pissed."

"Yes, I remember," said Rivera.

"Shit sucked, boss."

"I know, I know, Brown," replied Rivera as he placed his black CamelBak tube back in place. "The shakedown applied to me too, my friend."

"Well, that really bites, man. No McDonald's or Subway, no bowling alley, no gym or swimming pool, no beer drinking, no Windmill Beach, no Windjammer Club or Tiki Bar. Just stay within Camp America. Lockdown sucked royally, boss."

"Yes, it did, Brown."

"Four damn days of lockdown status," said Brown, "and of course no one had Lopez's nods. Me—I don't think they were stolen. Lopez lost them, pure and simple. That's what I think. Those nods could be anywhere."

"You might be right," Rivera said. "Lockdown and shakedown inspections are never fun, but maybe the soldier did lose his nods."

"And here's the worst part, boss: Lopez got promoted after that whole incident." Brown shook his head in frustration. "Dude loses his nods and gets promoted. That's so jacked up. It's fuck up, move up. That's how this shit-ding-Captain-Boswell operation works."

Rivera shifted on the footlocker to get more comfortable. He said, "Now, Brown, I know you got demoted, mi amigo, but I've seen improvement in you. Shit happens, son, but the key is how you deal with it. You can't get too pissed about some of the shit that's happened here." He paused for a couple of seconds.

"Sometimes, Brown, sometimes you just gotta suck it up and drive on."

Chapter 7

Sergeant First Class Rivera left Brown's tower at 0720 to check on the other towers. Brown, sitting on the wooden stool and scanning his sector, was looking out toward the southwest.

Less than two hours left on this shift, he thought. *Man, we're almost outta this joint.* He took a sip of Coke, and then he started thinking again about the cot layout of hooch 1305.

Let's see. Did Whitcomb, Bouchey, Python, Johnston, Rosey, and Blackwell. Who's next? He concentrated. *After Blackwell, it's Harrison. Then it's Mini Me. Then after that, it's Vega. My cot's after Vega's. Then the last cot directly across from Whitcomb's is Ralston's.*

Let's see. Harrison. Brown started thinking about Harrison as he kept scanning his sector.

Harrison's da man, the big staff sergeant, the big squad leader. Although Whitcomb was also a staff sergeant, Harrison had more time in rank, so that was why Harrison was the squad leader. *That's how the Army works, man. Rank has its privileges.*

Thinking about Harrison made Brown think of Johnny Python. Python could only hope and dream of being like Harrison. Harrison was a player. He couldn't help it. *Dude looks like a shorter version of Denzel Washington—muscular too, kinda like a Jamie Foxx type. Fact is, Harrison's got it: the bod, the looks, the voice, the moves. Ladies fall for Harrison—I've seen it at the Windjammer Club. The ladies go for Harrison—white chicks ... black Jamaican chicks ... it don't matter, man; they all fall for Harrison. Yeah, the dude's married, and he's got his wife and kids back in Amarillo, but I dunno if Da Man Harrison's been scoring down here at Gitmo—ain't my bizness, really. I'm sure he's had his chances, though. Me, I'm tight and loyal to Tywanna, but what other dudes do here is their bizness. As far as I'm concerned, what happens at Gitmo stays at Gitmo.*

Brown took another sip of Coke. He looked out at the clearly visible blue ocean, and toward the southeast he saw a white Coast Guard cutter heading west.

CHAPTER 8

Brown stood up, arched his back to stretch it, and then he took a sip of Coke. He looked slightly to his right to read the Tower Three graffiti again:

Stop-loss sucks.
ETS=FREEDOM.
Someone kill the hard charger!
GITMO—the least worst place.
I don't need Python pills—God gave me a BIG ONE.
Texas rules!
Twenty days and a wakeup.
For a good time and a BJ, call Joe at 7236.
Does Joe give good BJs?
If God loved gays, he would've created Adam and Steve.
Death to all Fags!
Jody got my bitch, but I'll get Jody when I return home.
666.
Jesus rules!
The real illegal immigrants came on the Mayflower.

He noted again that the three sixes were written in red ink and that *Jesus rules!* was written in black ink in someone else's handwriting.

He looked at his black Timex watch on his left wrist, seeing that it was 0750. *A little over an hour left,* he thought. He sat back on the wooden stool and resumed scanning his sector.

***

Brown saw something emerge out in the distance soon after calling in his 0800 radio check. Whatever he was looking at was near the Sea Galley mess hall. He focused and zeroed in.

Yep, here they come, all walkin' in neat rows to their job site, he thought. *Poor migrant workers. Them dudes work hard for those puny wages they's getting. Injustice right there, man. Big Halliburton should be paying 'em more. Better yet, 'em jobs should be going to Americans. Crap like that Pakistani worker leaving a shank behind wouldn't happen if the construction workers were Americans.*

He took another sip of Coke, and then he thought, *Okay, still got some time to kill.*

He quickly ran by his Big Four: *ETSing in April? Probably, man, probably. Convert to Islam? Yeah, probably a go on that one too. Pop the question to Tywanna? Yeah, that'd be cool. The package, man, the package. Wonder what the package is? Rolex? That'd be cool. I better get that package this morning. There's no telling what will happen to it here at Gitmo once I leave. Sure hope T got some insurance coverage on the package.*

He stood up while looking at the migrant workers heading toward Camp Delta.

Last dude I thought 'bout was Harrison. Following him is Mini Me Martin. Short dude's cool. Often hangs with Python. Hard worker. Knows everything 'bout the .50 caliber and shit. Sharp and quiet—that's Mini Me right there. Made corporal too—that was another rare, good promotion here at Gitmo.

He sat down on his tower stool.

Whitcomb sure deserved making staff sergeant, and Mini Me earned his corporal stripes, but other dudes—especially them broke dicks—didn't deserve their promotions. Me, fuck, man ... I got the reverse of a promotion. I got fuckin' demoted. Good old by-the-book Boswell. Dude's got it wrong. Shit don't matter much, though, 'cause I'm probably ETSing in April.

Brown looked at the approaching migrant workers dressed in their blue overalls, white hard hats, and beige work boots. He estimated they numbered around fifty. More would be coming to Camp Delta during the later morning hours. To the south, he could see the vast ocean, and miles away, on that vast ocean, he saw another white Coast Guard vessel, making a beeline for Gitmo.

He took a sip of Coke.

Okay, Mini Me. Dude's cool. I'm happy he made corporal. I'm sure he could use the extra pay. His wife is pregnant, he said. Dude's a butcher. Works in a grocery store. He told us Fifth Squadders that he makes decent money but he gets no benefits at the store. Shit, man, with his wife being pregnant, he told us he's kinda glad our unit got activated 'cause when you's on active duty, you get health care coverage for you and your dependents.

All right, who's next? Vega. Yeah, it's Vega 'cause his cot is next to Mini Me's. Vega, man, he's a Jesus freak, but I like him anyway. I know he ain't too crazy 'bout me maybe converting to Islam and all, but shit, you gotta do what you gotta do. Vega's cool, man. Another hard worker. Prison guard in civilian life. Left Commie Central America for greener pastures here in Uncle Sugar's land.

Brown interlaced his fingers and cracked his knuckles. He felt his shirt sticking to his back. *Damn, it's getting hotter and more humid by the minute now that the sun's up.* He grabbed his Coke can with his right hand. He shrugged. *Alrighty, who's next? After Vega, it's my cot, then it's Ralston. Yeah, Ralston's the last Fifth Squadder.*

Brown thought about Ralston's height. He was probably six feet six, if not taller. Brown knew Ralston was taller than Johnston, who was six feet five.

Poor Ralston, man. Like some other 2-142 dudes, he's got bad feet, which explains why he's got that foot profile. What else? Well, like Blackwell, Ralston's taking a big pay cut by being on active duty. Ralston's a cook—actually, I think he's a chef—back home. Makes serious bank at it too.

Man, that cooking stuff reminds me when we had 'em hurricane warnings back in August. Shit, all of Camp America was evacuated and moved to downtown Gitmo 'cause of 'em high winds. Brown remembered that most of the guys from hooch 1305 had stayed in an Air Force officer's house. Ralston had really showed off his cooking skills. *Baked breads, soufflés, steaks, pastas, all the fixings—you name it, Ralston cooked it. It was awesome, man.*

Brown stood up. He quickly did a few toe touches to stretch his back, and then he sat back down and resumed scanning his sector.

What else 'bout Ralston? Big dude, quiet, broke dick 'cause of the foot profile, watches lots of free flicks at the lyceum. What else? Oh shit—how the fuck can I forget? The thinking is Ralston's gay—lots of us Fifth Squadders think he's gay. Me, I think he is, and it don't bother me any. You's queer, you's queer. So he's a flamer—big deal. Or maybe he's a switch-hitter, a bisexual. Who knows? Who gives a fuck, really? I know Islam don't look too favorably on the gay thing, but shit, man, to me it's all biological—sexuality's biological. We's all born a certain way.

Ya know, that homo stuff gets me thinking 'bout how tight we is in Fifth Squad. I'm sure of this: If gay Ralston ever got himself in a fight here at Gitmo, I know we Fifth Squadders would come to his defense. We'd cover his back—no questions asked. Heck, there's a saying: "Ain't no atheists in foxholes." In my opinion, ain't no bigots or homophobes in 'em neither. One team, one fight. I'll face you, man.

CHAPTER 9

In late October of 2002, just a week after Brown had visited Tywanna and her family during the ten-day R & R, Tonya Banks had invited her younger sister, Tywanna, for a girls' night out.

"Let's go clubbing, T—it'll be fun, sis," she had told Tywanna. "It's Friday night, girl. Ya know them clubs here in Amarillo are hopping on Friday nights."

"I don't know, Ton. I'm kinda tired right now. Besides, who'll watch Danielle?"

"Oh, girl, Mama will take care of Danielle. C'mon, it'll be fun—coupla drinks and dancin'."

"But I'm always asking Mama for—"

"Relax, girl. Mama loves watching Danielle. Besides, T, Shayna and Liz said they'd tag along. C'mon, girls' night out. I won't drink too much ... so I'll drive. Hell, girl, I know how much you like dancin'."

"All right ... okay, but we don't stay out too late," Tywanna had said, "because I start work at nine tomorrow morning."

CHAPTER 10

Brown kept scanning his sector and occasionally sipping Coke. His Big Four was on his mind.

ETS coming up. Yeah, I think it's time to throw in the towel, report to Fort Living Room, and become a full-time civilian.

Pop the question to T? Yeah, I think we're both ready to tie the knot. The big C, man—commitment. Heck, I really didn't get a chance to ask Tywanna to marry me back in October 'cause we was too busy and shit during my R & R.

Become a Muslim? I feel it, man. Islam's straightening me out. Plus, T's cool with Islam.

And then the most immediate of his Big Four: *God, I hope that package comes in this morning. I'll soon find out. Who knows—maybe I'll be flying back to Texas today with a Rolex on my wrist. That be cool shit right there.*

Brown shifted on his stool, and as he did, something caught his eye, something toward the west. Something like a flash and spark. He turned in that direction and saw one of the migrant workers welding.

Hell, 'em welding sparks always look like the flash of a camera, and cameras and photos ain't allowed here. Welding sparks always throw me off, man.

He took a sip of Coke, and then he looked at his watch; it read 8:27. *'bout thirty minutes to go. I can't wait to get outta here.* He stood up. *Our last shift, man. Shit's finally over.* He was both tired and happy—tired from working a long shift, and happy it was his last one.

He started pacing around Tower Three, and to kill some time, he decided to go over his squad buddies again.

Staff Sergeant Whitcomb. Squared-away fella. Good promotion—he deserved it.

Bouchey, the law student who hopes to get in the JAG Corps. Introduced me to Grisham books.

Pussy-chasing Python. Horny dude, man. All open with his shit. Too bad 'bout that DUI stuff; too bad he ain't on that plane with us later today.

Johnston. Tall, great athlete. Thanks for pulling me outta that fight, bro.

Rosey. Never thought he'd deploy with us 'cause of that banged-up leg. Good luck with becoming a Lubbock cop, and keep ridin' 'em motorcycles, but be careful, dude.

Blackwell. Good old West Texas boy. Broke peanut farmer. Better at manager of a peanut wholesale business. Sucks he took a pay cut 'cause of this deployment. Good luck fighting the IRS, and take care of 'em feet.

Harrison. The sharp-dressed brother. Muscular. Football coach. Thanks for giving me tips here and there like "Don't drink too much, bro; keep your nose clean."

Mini Me. Good little hard charger right there. Good promotion to corporal. Good luck with the newborn.

Vega. Jesus freak, but you's cool, man. I'm glad you and your family are in Uncle Sugar's land. Christians and Muslims can get along—for real.

And Ralston. Thanks for that great chow, that great grub back during those hurricane-warning days. I don't care if you's a homo, man. And take care of those feet—or as Johnston puts it, "those Japanese jump boots."

Brown smiled. *Ah, man, the dudes of Fifth Squad. Shit, you spend some eight months with a group of fellas, and you get to know them and—*

"Attention, all 2-142 soldiers. This is the SOG."

It was Harrison's voice over the Saber radio. Brown looked at his watch, which read 8:35, and wondered if it was an early radio check.

"Y'all will soon be relieved by our replacements from the Virginia National Guard," Harrison said over the radio. "Don't forget to bring your tower logs, binos, used Saber battery, compass, and personal items. This will serve as your final radio check. Commence final radio checks in sequence at this time."

Brown heard Rosey say "Tower Two" over the Saber radio.

He followed with, "Tower Three."

Then came Johnston with, "Tower Four—yahoo! Fort Hood and deactivation, here we come!"

"Maintain your composure, Tower Four," said Harrison. "Keep your head in the game. We ain't home yet."

"That's a big ten-four," Johnston replied over the radio.

The other 2-142 soldiers called in their radio checks, and then Harrison followed with, "Roger, 2-142 soldiers, that's a good copy. Reminder for y'all: bring your stuff to the QRF trailer and properly brief your replacements. Good shift, men. SOG out."

Brown walked over to the large footlocker occupying the center of Tower Three. He leaned over and picked up both the 1561 tower log form and his range card, placing these next to his TA-50 gear. Inside the footlocker, he noticed a hammer, a huge adjustable wrench, a Phillips screwdriver, and a pack of sandpaper. He didn't know who put those things in there; he hadn't used them.

Cling clang cling, he heard just as he was about to turn around and head back to his stool. By the sound, he knew someone was climbing his tower, someone whose M16 was hitting the metal ladder. *Probably my replacement*, he thought. He walked to the tower entrance, where the tip of the tower ladder met the plywood floor. He peeked down.

Yep, soldier I don't recognize, he thought. *Dude's got his full battle rattle on—ruck, M16, binos, K-pot, CamelBak. Cool, man, my replacement.*

"Morning," said the soldier, who was almost at the top of the ladder.

"Morning," replied Brown.

"Thanks, PFC," said the soldier as Brown extended his hand to help him step onto the tower floor. "I'm Specialist McElroy from the Virginia National Guard. I'm here to replace you."

"Roger that," said Brown as he released McElroy's hand. "Welcome to Tower Three of Camp Delta." Brown noticed the soldier's face was red and sweaty. *Dude's pudgy too*, he thought.

McElroy took a quick sip of water from his CamelBak, which was hugging his upper back. He then started placing his equipment in the southwestern portion of the tower, the portion where Brown's stuff was.

"How long have you guys been here?" he asked as he started removing his TA-50 gear.

"Six months, man," said Brown, who was still standing next to the tower entrance. "We trained six weeks at Fort Hood before coming here … so 'bout eight months in all."

"Six months, huh?" said McElroy. "Well, at least you guys will be home for Christmas. What a jacked-up schedule our unit has. Setting foot on Gitmo in mid-December. Shit blows."

Brown replied, "I hear you." Then he said, "Well, lemme show you 'round here."

"Great," said McElroy.

"Well, as you can see, we've got these arrows carved in ink in this wood pole here. South is the ocean. Southwest you'll see Camp America." Brown then pointed. "And next to Camp America is the Sea Galley mess hall. See: *N* for north, *S* for south, and so on."

"Got it," said McElroy. "Hey, how's the chow here, anyway?"

"In a word: chicken," said Brown. "That's what they serve almost all the time. No AC in there either, but they've got these huge-ass fans blowing all the time. Damn things make so much noise, but at least it keeps the place cool some. Hard as heck to carry on a conversation in the mess hall 'cause those fans make so much noise. Napkins fly by too sometimes."

"Sweet," said McElroy as he rolled his eyes. He walked over to the footlocker and sat on it. "Man, this is a large footlocker." He thumped it. "What is this? Plastic? No problem, right, if I sit on this thing?"

"Sure, no prob," Brown said. "Everybody sits on it. It's mostly empty, but it contains a few tools and shit. It don't belong to our unit. We also have the stool to sit on."

"Oh, I see that. Cool."

McElroy got himself comfortable on the footlocker, and as he did he caught a glimpse of one of the tower plywood walls.

"Daaaaaaaaaaaamn," he said in amazement. "Holy crap. There's a lot of graffiti on that wall." He read out loud, "For a good time and a BJ call Joe at 7236. Ah, that shit's sick. Fuck that sick homo shit."

Brown smiled, and then he proceeded to mention a few things to McElroy, like how he sometimes mistook the migrant workers' welding sparks for camera flashes, the hours of operation at the bowling alley, all about the Windjammer Club and the Tiki Bar, the fact that there are plenty of iguanas and banana rats on Gitmo, how to be careful driving a Humvee over certain narrow Gitmo roads. "And some outfit offers scuba diving certification classes over at Windmill Beach," Brown finally informed McElroy.

"Cooooooool," replied McElroy. "Hey, I just might sign up for that."

Brown started gathering his stuff. He walked over to one of the tower's support beams and removed his CamelBak hanging from a nail. He then walked back to the corner of the tower where his TA-50 gear was. He started putting on his flak vest and TA-50 gear.

"You were right, PFC, when you told me there were plenty of iguanas and rats here on Gitmo, because I've already seen tons of them," McElroy said. He was still sitting on the footlocker.

"Yep, sure are," responded Brown as he slung his M16 over his right shoulder. "Like I told you, 'em rats are called banana rats. Why the name banana rats, I dunno, but I know they's everywhere. They come out feeding at night."

"They look a lot like possums," said McElroy. "We have lots of possums in Virginia, and they look like that."

Brown then chimed in with, "And guess what, Specialist? The federal government hired this hunter dude to kill lots of 'em banana rats here 'cause they ruin the vegetation. You'll see that hunter dude from time to time."

"You're shitting me, right?"

"Nah, man. For real."

"Man, that's a job I wish I had," said McElroy. "Getting paid to hunt. That would be the life."

Brown gathered his equipment and tossed his empty Coke can in the black plastic garbage bag near the footlocker. He was about ready to descend the ladder when he asked McElroy, "You good on everything? Binos? Compass? Tower logs?"

"All set, PFC," McElroy said confidently. "Our first sergeant is coming to do his rounds later this morning. That's when we'll be issued all the equipment. Fan and footlocker stay here right?"

"Roger that," said Brown, and just as he spoke, a thought hit him: "Uh, Specialist McElroy? Can I get your John Hancock on this form?" Brown needed to document that he had been properly relieved of tower guard duty.

"Sure."

Brown got out the tower log he had recently stuffed in his rucksack. He pulled out a pen from his left BDU pocket, and then he wrote the following on the log form: I, PFC Brown of the 2-142, was relieved of tower guard duty by SPC McElroy of the VA NG. He initialed the entry and wrote the time of 0855. He then handed the log form for McElroy to initial.

"Bet you're glad to get outta here, huh?" said McElroy as he initialed the log form. He gave Brown the form and his pen back.

"You know it, Specialist," said Brown as he repacked the tower log in his ruck and started descending the metal ladder.

***

Five minutes later, Brown entered the QRF trailer, and once inside, he immediately saw Third Squad members busily sweeping and mopping floors and organizing green Army cots along the hallway walls.

He started walking down the hallway and almost immediately saw Sergeant First Class Rivera standing next to the big white planning board hanging from the wall on the east side. Harrison, Rosey, and Johnston, were there too, handing their tower logs to Rivera. In the background, Brown saw Ralston—all six and a half feet of him—mopping a floor.

"Mornin', boss," Brown greeted Rivera. "I just got relieved of tower duty. I'm ready to get outta this joint." He saw Harrison, Rosey, and Johnston leave the QRF trailer.

"Roger, mi amigo," said the short bespectacled Rivera. He was erasing names from the planning board behind him. "Got all your shit, Brown?"

"Roger, boss. Compass, binos, tower log, my TA-50, and my weapon, of course. All set and at the ready."

"What about batteries, Brown? Did you exchange Saber batteries with your replacement?"

Brown shook his head in frustration. "Ah, sorry, boss." His tone was a disappointed one. "I just left the Saber radio at the tower. I don't know if my replacement has a charged-up battery for it."

"No problemo, mi amigo," replied Rivera earnestly. "You're not the only one. That's their unit's problem if they don't tell their soldiers to bring fresh batteries when they go on guard duty."

Brown placed his compass, binoculars, and tower log on the small metal table next to Rivera. Rivera quickly inspected and inventoried the items.

"You're all set, Brown," he said after his cursory inspection. "Good job. Just get on the deuce and a half with your squad and head over to Camp A."

"That's a big ten-four, boss."

Brown, still carrying his M16 and dressed in his battle rattle, exited the QRF trailer and immediately took a sharp right. Next to the north fence line of Camp Delta, he could see the beige metal water tank, and next to that, he saw the old green deuce-and-a-half truck that was parked but idling.

As he walked toward the truck, he noticed Whitcomb in the cab behind the wheel. Vega and Mini Me sat in the truck's flatbed. Vega called to him. "Lemme help you. It's hard to climb aboard wearing that heavy rucksack."

As Brown stood at the base of the truck's bed near the left rear wheel, Vega extended his right hand, and Brown grabbed it. He stepped on the truck's left back tire and propelled himself forward as Vega pulled him toward the truck bed.

"Thanks, bro," said Brown as soon as his feet were firmly planted on the wooden truck bed. He walked to the right front corner, put down his rucksack, and then sat on his rucksack. In less than five minutes, all the rest of the Fifth Squaders were sitting in the truck bed.

"Everybody up? Everybody got all their shit?" asked Harrison as he removed his earpieces. He was standing on the flatbed next to the truck's cab.

Every Fifth Squader nodded or gave Harrison the thumbs-up. Then Harrison struck the top hood of the truck's cab a couple of times—the cue for Whitcomb to pull out and start driving.

As the truck started moving slowly, Brown, sitting on his rucksack, observed his fellow Fifth Squaders: *Vega's reading a pocket-size Bible; Bouchey's reading a Grisham novel; Harrison, with earpieces, is listening to some tunes, probably rap; Johnston and Rosey are chitchatting about bikes and chicks. Mini Me's quiet.*

***

Ten minutes later, the truck reached Camp America and was parked at its normal parking spot—directly next to the 2-142 equipment supply CONEX.

Brown stood up, and as he did, he instantly saw the big rock next to the CONEX. *Hell, that's the rock where Sergeant Adams almost ended his life; it's where he sat and chain-smoked, his loaded M16 within arm's reach of him.*

"All right, move out! Move out, Fifth Squad," yelled Harrison. "We ain't got all day, fellas. We've got lots of packing and shit to do."

The men bunched up, ready to jump off the truck. Harrison yelled, "Y'all better watch your friggin' step off this truck. Remember Alvarez in Second Platoon? Hotshot space cadet sprained his ankle real fucking fine by jumping off this same truck."

Brown stopped and listened.

"Injury cost him four days of work," Harrison continued. "That's four days when somebody else in your squad or platoon has to cover for your ass and work your shift. Don't fuck your battle buddy by trying to be Superman and jump off this truck. Hell, we already have enough broke dicks in this unit, and none of you need an injury on our way home for Christmas. Y'all know the deal, fellas—ground your ruck first, then step off the truck. No jumping off. Everybody tracking?"

Everyone said yes, nodded in approval, or gave Harrison the thumbs-up.

"Good," said Harrison. "Y'all move out!"

The Fifth Squadders all got off the truck's flatbed per Harrison's guidance: they first threw their heavy rucksacks on the ground, and then, one by one, each carefully placed his feet on the truck's rear tires for step supports while holding on to the side rails to guide his descent to the ground.

"You guys know the deal: if you think your weapon's clean, then turn it in now in the CONEX," Harrison said in a commanding voice as the Fifth Squadders were still getting off the truck. "Blackwell and some of the other high-speed broke dicks are in the CONEX to inspect your weapons. Otherwise, if your weapon ain't clean, which it probably ain't, then start cleaning it either on the picnic table next to the CONEX or back in our hooch. Again, y'all know the deal—treat this like a regular shift change."

Once they got off the truck and picked up their rucksacks, the Fifth Squadders headed toward their hooch because that was the norm: every one of them usually cleaned his M16 in the hooch because it was cool there, whereas the outdoor picnic table was always hot and humid. Plus, Rosey often played a porno DVD on his DVD player while the squad cleaned their weapons in hooch 1305, and porn was something the Fifth Squadders, save the religious Vega, always looked forward to.

After some thirty seconds of walking, Vega and Brown approached the two Camp America latrine sheds. Brown noticed PFC Reid, a 2-142 soldier from Second Platoon, standing next to the outdoor covered sinks. Nineteen-year-old Reid, one of the youngest 2-142 members, was wearing his TA-50 gear and Kevlar; his M16 was slung over his right shoulder. He also had an all-too-familiar lit cigarette pursed between his lips.

"Morning, dudes," Reid said as Brown and Vega approached. Brown immediately stopped walking, while Vega and the other Fifth Squadders kept heading toward hooch 1305. Brown decided to kill some time. His stuff was already packed, and his weapon wasn't too dirty. *Besides*, he thought, *the mail don't arrive till ten thirty or so. I'll chitchat a bit with Reid. Dude's funny too—I could use a laugh.*

"I see you ain't quit those cancer sticks, Reid," Brown said as he placed his heavy rucksack on the small crushed rocks next to the latrines and outdoor sinks. The two shook hands.

"Ah, Brown, you know me," said Reid. "I'm a good soldier—I ain't a quitter."

"I see that," said Brown, shaking his head in disapproval. "But you best be thinkin' of cutting back. Next thing you know, the big C will catch up with you—cancer, man."

"Well, Brown, I'll take my chances." He took a slow drag.

"Well, we made it, stud," Brown said as he placed his hands comfortably on his M16 that was still slung over his right shoulder. "This Gitmo mission is winding down, buddy. We's in Texas tonight."

"Amen to that," Reid said. He quickly exhaled some smoke. "Brown, buddy, I can't wait to get back, especially since my grandma's not doing too hot. She just got done with gall bladder surgery. I plan on seeing her during Christmas for sure."

"That's cool, man," responded Brown.

A few quiet seconds passed, and then Reid said, "Hey, Brown, gotta good one for ya."

"Fire away," Brown said, thinking, *I figured Reid would tell me a joke.*

"It's a lawyer joke. Friend sent it to me over the Internet last week."

"Lawyer joke will do, bro."

"All right," said Reid. He took a quick puff and exhaled some smoke. "See, Brown, there was this dude, right, and he goes to this bar. As soon as he enters the bar, he sees a nice chick sitting at the bar. Chick's a real hottie, and this dude really wants her, so he goes over to her and says, 'Can I buy you a drink?' Hot chick says sure, so he sits next to her and orders a couple of drinks. Bartender brings the drinks, and the two start drinking; then the hot chick asks the dude, 'So, what do you do for a livin'?' The dude says, 'I'm a lawyer.' Hot chick then says, 'A lawyer—that's nice. You must make a lot of money.' The lawyer dude picks up his courage, right, and then he says, 'Yeah, I make good money—good enough to pay for a room in that fancy hotel across the street. How about me and you go over there and get busy?' Hot chick knows she's hot, and she wants some action too, so she says, 'Sure, honey.' So the two pound their drinks down and head over to the hotel across the street. They get a room, and they start doing the wild thing, right. A quickie was what it was, and while they were doing it, the lawyer dude had this big cocky smile on his face, and he was laughing too. The hot chick asks him, 'Why are you smiling and laughing?' And that's when the lawyer dude looks her straight in the eye and says, 'Oh yeah, I'm a lawyer all right. I've only known you for fifteen minutes, and I'm already screwing you.'"

Brown chuckled. "That's a good one, Reid."

"Thanks." He puffed on his cigarette again and exhaled. "I figured you'd like it."

Brown picked up his rucksack with his right arm and started walking toward hooch 1305. "Gotta go, Reid. I'll see you on that chartered bird later this afternoon."

***

Brown reached the front steps of hooch 1305 in less than a minute. The wooden steps were worn and splintered in places. A couple of the steps were busted. Brown was glad not to have to go up and down those steps much longer. As he placed his hand on the railing, a thought hit him: *Heck, cleaning my weapon ain't nothing but a thing. It'll take me just five minutes to clean it. Besides, my shit's already packed. Maybe it's best I try calling Tywanna now—yeah, I've got time to call her. And the package ... Shit, man, mail won't come for another hour or so. I still got some time to call my T.*

Still carrying his full load of gear and his weapon, Brown turned to the right and started walking on the dirt pathway separating hooches 1305 and 1307. He eyed the small building that contained computer stations and telephones. He thought about how nice it was to have a computer room and phones right behind their hooch.

He climbed the front steps of the computer room's wood deck and then turned the corner to the right to use one of the outside-mounted phones and ... *Ah fuck. Figures*, he thought. He counted at least five soldiers behind each of the three phones. *Man, I've got time but not that much time.* Telephone honor policy was fifteen minutes max per phone call. *With five or six dudes behind every phone, that'll take at least an hour.*

He slowly swept sweat off his forehead with the back of his right hand.

Crap, it woulda been good to speak to T. Oh well, as long as I'm here I might as well check the computer room. When's the last time I e-mailed Tywanna? Two ... no, it was three days ago; it was just after vehicle checkpoints. Yeah, three days ago.

T had e-mailed me saying she sent me a package. Said she sent it DHL. I e-mailed her back saying I hope I get it before I leave this joint.

Brown took half a dozen steps forward on the wood deck, then he turned right and opened the front door to the computer room. He walked in. *Ah, man, that AC sure feels good.*

The computer room was just like the wooden hooches of Camp America, only bigger. It was entirely made of two-by-fours and plywood. A large air-conditioning unit kept the room cool (it was surprisingly quiet even when running), and two plain but long tables lined two of the inside walls. Five computers had been placed on each table.

Brown took a few steps to his left, and then he placed his rucksack on an empty space on the floor. Next to follow were his Kevlar and TA-50 gear, which he also placed on the floor. He kept his M16 slung over his right shoulder.

Nice. Better luck here 'cause no one's waiting to get on a computer, and I see one available. He walked over to the unoccupied computer, he sat in the gray metal chair in front of it, and he proceeded to ...

"Dude, that piece of crap ain't working," said a soldier to Brown's right. Brown quickly turned and looked at the soldier.

"Thanks, man," said Brown. He didn't recognize the soldier sitting at the next station. "I'll just wait till a computer opens up."

"Well, I'm almost finished using mine," said the soldier. "Just a coupla more words to type on this e-mail ..." He started typing. "And ... there. Finished. Hit the Send button, and ... there. All yours." The soldier got up.

"Thanks," said Brown. He took the soldier's seat and grabbed the mouse. *Thank God for e-mail*, he thought. *It's the best way to keep in touch with Tywanna.*

He moved the cursor to the Internet Explorer icon, double-clicked, and quickly typed his Yahoo! e-mail username and password. The Yahoo! screen popped up right away.

Twenty-seven messages in my in-box, he thought. *All junk.*
He started scanning down the message senders. *Junk, junk, junk.* He started checking off and hitting the Delete button as he scrolled down the junk e-mails, one by one. *Ah, but here's two messages from my T.* He smiled and double-clicked on the first of T's e-mails.

Hi, babe. Hope you're well. Me and Danielle miss you lots. I won't make this too long cuz I'm busy with a lot of things right now, including the holiday shopping. I know you can't wait to get out of Cuba, and we're so anxious to see you. Hope you have a good flight to Fort Hood. Call me when you get there. Kisses, T.

Hmm, thought Brown. *Nice e-mail, but she didn't mention nothing 'bout the package.*

He hit the Delete button and opened the next e-mail from Tywanna.

Hey, stud. Hey, baby. How's it hanging? Good, I hope. Hey, did you get my package? You should've cuz I sent it DHL (yeah, cost me lots, but it was worth it). DHL promised me you'd get it by tomorrow morning ...

Wondering when this e-mail was sent, he immediately checked the date. It was sent yesterday. He finished reading the e-mail.

Hope you like the package, baby—I know I did. Kisses, T.

Smiling, he clicked the Reply button and typed:

T baby, just got off my last shift—yeah, I can hardly believe it. Mail usually comes in the morning, in about an hour, so I haven't seen the package yet, but if you sent it DHL, then I should get it. I miss you and Danielle lots. I'll be at Fort Hood, Texas, tonight. I'll call.

Kisses from me,
JB
P.S. I can't wait to open the package—I think I know what it is.

He hit the Send button, logged off, picked up his gear, and headed out the door.

***

As soon as he entered hooch 1305, Brown noticed Rosey and Johnston in the far right corner, checking out a porno DVD while cleaning their M16s. He also noticed that the entire squad, save Blackwell and Ralston, was in the hooch and that everyone's M16 was disassembled with small parts spread out on top of every cot. Harrison, having a boom box on a wooden shelf over his cot, was listening to tunes through his earphones. The other Fifth Squadders were laughing, talking about Christmas travel plans, and cleaning their M16s. Occasionally, they would look in the others' direction to catch a glimpse of the porno.

Brown walked to his cot—the second one to the left, between Ralston's and Vega's. He placed his ruck, Kevlar, and TA-50 gear on his cot, and then he walked a few paces to the brown mini refrigerator between Python's and Johnston's cots. He opened the refrigerator door and got himself a water bottle. He then slowly walked back to his cot and sat on it, and just as he was about to start disassembling his M16, the front door opened.

It was Staff Sergeant Grazdan, a well-respected noncommissioned officer responsible for all pay, travel, mail, and other paperwork issues for the unit. He served as the unofficial postmaster general. "Morning, y'all," Grazdan said in his West Texas drawl. "Last mail call, gang. Mail's a bit early today."

Brown opened his water bottle and took a gulp.

"Just got mail for Brown and Python this morning," Grazdan said as he walked over to Python. "Here you go, stud."

94

He handed him a small package. "It's probably more of your love letters from those fuck magazines. And speaking of fuck magazines, I see Rosey and Johnston are heavily indulged in some viewing pleasure."

"Roger that, big sarge," responded Rosey, smiling. "Hey, gotta keep the troops motivated. I'm glad I brought my DVD player to Gitmo."

"I see that," said the tall and balding Grazdan. "But y'all make sure to use that TSP oil to lubricate your weapons and not your love sticks. Everybody tracking?"

A couple of the Fifth Squadders laughed. Johnston said, "Roger, Sergeant. We're not all like Python." Python, unaware of what had just been said, was busy opening his mail.

Grazdan turned and headed toward the front door, and as he did, he tossed a small package on Brown's cot.

"For you, JB. Sent DHL. That shit ain't cheap, you know. Must be something important."

"Thanks," said Brown, but his tone was unenthused. The package, if you could call it that, was just a plain yellow envelope. He could tell there was no way he was getting a Rolex. *This is the package?* he thought. *It's a flat envelope, man.*

"I'll see y'all on that chartered bird this afternoon," said Grazdan, and he headed out the front door of the hooch.

Brown, sitting on his cot, thought, *An envelope, man. I expected something bigger.* He unslung his M16 and placed it on his cot, and then he started tearing at the taped edges of the yellow envelope. *Wonder what's in here.* He continued removing clear packaging tape. *Photos?*

Instinctively, he flipped the envelope to check its back side. *Yep, sure is. Says* DO NOT BEND. *I'm guessing it's photos. When's the last time me and Tywanna took photos? Maybe she's just sending photos of herself and Danielle.*

He kept struggling with the tightly taped edges of the envelope. In the background, he heard, "Wow, check out the rack on that babe! That chick's got huge melons." It was Johnston's voice, followed by Rosey saying, "Hu-wee, yeah, man. She's getting it from behind too. Hey, Python, come here and check out the porn."

Brown noticed Python leaving his cot to join the DVD viewing. He also saw Harrison and Mini Me doing the same.

Man, Tywanna sure taped this bad boy like she didn't want anyone to open it ... Hmm? I don't remember taking photos with T back in October—we was too busy. It's probably photos of T with Danielle. That's cool.

"Yeah, now they're two-timing her. Giddy up, cowboys. It's slam-bangin' time."

Brown struggled with the taped envelope. *Photos. Must be photos of T and Danielle.* He finally was able to peel off one of the taped edges. *There—got it.* He removed a pen from his BDU pocket and used it to slice the remaining tape off the envelope.

"Yee-haw. Humpa-humpa. Attaboy—you go, stud. Bang that chick, man." That was Johnston again, commenting on the viewing pleasure. Brown saw Johnston high-fiving Python.

With the envelope now open, Brown attempted to empty its contents by turning the envelope upside down. *Not working ... Yep, I see—it's photos all right.* Brown peeked inside. *Photos in there are tight—looks like Polaroids too.* He placed his right thumb and right index finger through the open slit and managed to remove a photo, and then he turned the envelope upside down again, and this time three photos fell on his cot. Brown peeked inside the envelope. There was nothing more inside.

"Hey, Brown, come check out the porn, bro." That was Harrison speaking. "Chick's real fine, bro."

"Maybe later, fellas," said Brown. "Checking my mail here."

Brown looked down at the three photos on his cot: one was right side up, the other two were facedown. He looked at the photo he held with his right thumb and index fingers.

What the ...? What the ...? Oh ... oh ... Oh God, oh Lord ... Lord, no ... No! Oh ... no! Not me, Lord. He felt his heart pound. His face felt hot. A warm feeling—an oozing feeling—started from his throat and worked down to the pit of his stomach. *No! No! Not me. Not me, God! No way ... this ... this can't ... oh ... no.* His heart raced. His chest felt tight. His face was flushed.

He picked up the other three photos. They were similar to the first one. He noticed the photos were shaking because his hands were shaking. *Oh ... no. No! Not me, Lord. Not me!*

He felt as if he couldn't breathe. He wanted to swallow just to calm himself, but he couldn't because his chest was so tight. *Heart racing. Face hot. Chest tight.* He yelled, "Fuckin' bitch! Goddamn fuckin' bitch!" Heavy breathing. The warm oozing feeling all over. Heart pounding. He stood up from his cot. "King Kong ain't got nothing on me!"

All the Fifth Squadders were looking at him. Johnston finally asked, "Brown, you okay, bro?"

Brown picked up his M16. Holding it made him feel better. With his TA-50 gear on his cot, he reached for one of the ammo pouches and removed a thirty-round magazine.

The DVD kept playing, but everyone was staring at Brown. Noises of the porn actors could be heard in the background.

"I'm fine, Johnston, just fine," Brown said in a surprisingly calm tone, even though he was breathing heavily. He pulled the charging handle, quickly locked the bolt to the rear, and inserted the magazine. He let the bolt go forward. "Locked, cocked, and ready to rock. I'm an owl, man, and I'm looking for a big-ass moth to eat. Just like Teddy Roosevelt too. Time to kick butt and take names later."

He saw the Fifth Squadders staring. He said, "Yo yo yo, fellas—Big Dawg here. But don't none of you worry; I won't go postal. I do want y'all outta this hooch, though, 'cept of course for our beloved squad leader, Brother Harrison."

Whitcomb, standing in the corner next to his cot, said, "Brown, put the weapon down. Put the fucking weapon down, Brown."

Smiling, Brown turned to Whitcomb and said, "Nah. Me and Harrison need to have ourselves a little man-to-man talk." Then Brown looked at Johnston and the others and said, "Y'all need to get out of this hooch. I mean it, fellas. Ain't no fuckin' with me no more."

Python suddenly started turning white. Vega, only some eight feet to the left of Brown, clearly wanted to say something, but the words weren't coming out. Brown noticed Vega's lower lip quivering.

"Don't worry, my Christian buddy. Everything's gonna be okay, Vega. I know you ain't crazy 'bout me converting to Islam, but I wouldn't hurt you, bro. I just need to have me a good talk with our squad leader."

Brown pointed his weapon at Harrison, who stood stone-faced. "I told y'all to get the fuck out. I'm serious, man. Just me and Harrison in our little hooch."

"Brown, don't get crazy now," Johnston said in a hurried and nervous tone. "Don't do anything to—"

"Shut up, Johnston," snapped Brown. "Just do as I say. Y'all just leave through the back door. Sorry I had to cut short your porn viewing, but y'all know how it is—bizness is bizness."

Harrison took a step forward. "Now, Brown, I—"

"Shut up! Me and you will talk in just a sec when everybody's out. Oh, and Rosey, buddy, why don't you turn that DVD off. I got enough distractions now."

Rosey turned off the DVD. Vega rushed toward the back door.

"Now that's a good boy, Vega," said Brown, nodding in approval. "Y'all follow his lead now." He kept his M16 pointed at Harrison.

A few quiet seconds passed, and then Brown yelled, "Out, fellas! Out!" He took two steps forward. When Johnston moved toward Harrison, Brown said, "I knows you's smart, Johnston, but don't try anything funny. Don't be protecting Harrison. Don't be a hero. Y'all just leave the hooch now."

No one moved.

"Fuck it!"

Brown aimed at the hooch's wooden ceiling. He pulled the trigger. *Pow!* The shot was deafening in the small confines of the hooch. "Yep, my M16's workin' just fine, fellas."

Python's entire body shook. Johnston and Rosey looked stunned. Whitcomb froze in his tracks. Mini Me froze like a brick, plainly wanting to run but unable to. Harrison's body was rigid.

Brown took two steps forward. "Out. Everybody out 'cept Harrison."

Vega had been the first to exit through the back door. Now Rosey did the same, then Johnston, then Mini Me, followed by Python and Whitcomb.

"Hey, Whitcomb, buddy, close the door, man," said Brown as Whitcomb walked out of the hooch. Whitcomb did as he was told and closed the door.

"Brown, put the weapon down," said Harrison, his voice shaky but audible. Brown was some ten feet away and still pointing his M16 at him.

"What the fuck, bro?" said Brown. He felt sweat running down his forehead. "What up, man?"

"Brown, put the weapon down."

"Shit, ya know what this is 'bout," said Brown.

"Brown, I swear I—"

"You swear jack shit, man! Brother, how could you? You of all people—the squad leader, the role model and shit. How could you, man?"

"Brown, I swear I didn't—"

"You didn't what? Say it!" He took another step toward Harrison.

Harrison was silent, and stiff.

"That's right, bro. You ain't got nothin' to say. Fuck, man, you of all people. Fuck, man, everybody knows the hard charger chose a nigga like you to look over my black ass after he busted me in rank. You gave me tips, helped me out, covered my back and flanks. How could ya—"

"Brown, I swear we were all fucked up. Drugs, man. I swear. Somebody spiked my drink or some shit. I know I toked a bit on some weed. Fuck, we ain't doing urinalysis tests here, so I decided to party. I swear I didn't know she was ... she ... I didn't know where I was or what the fuck took place, man."

99

Brown narrowed his eyes. Harrison clenched his fists. "You gotta believe me, bro—somebody drugged me up real good. I swear on my wife and kids that I didn't know what the fuck was going on. Later I found out, but I figured you wouldn't know ... and that it was better for me not to—"

"Shut up, man. Shut up." Brown felt that warm feeling again—like warm blood pumping throughout him. His heart was pounding again.

"Fuckin' nigga! Fuck you!"

"Brown, I ..."

Brown zoned out. Harrison was speaking, but Brown was overwhelmed by his thoughts:

Tywanna, the photos, Harrison—how could he? The e-mail: Hey, did you get my package? Nothing makes sense. Pain, hurt, injustice.

"... and I promise, Brown, I swear that ..."

Pain, injustice. Shit hurts.

He heard loud knocking on the front door ... then a voice through a bullhorn: "Private First Class Brown, come out with your hands up so we can see them. This is Captain Boswell. Your hooch is surrounded by armed MPs. Come out with your hands up."

Harrison's talking, but I ain't hearing; pain, hurt, betrayal. I've got nothing, man, nothing. Shit's all jacked up. Shit makes no sense. Why the fuck would Tywanna ... Harrison ... I'm hurting. Oh God, shit really hurts, man. I can't breathe. Shit, why me, God?

"Brown, I swear I ..."

Photos. Shit hurts. I don't get it. Shit makes no sense. Heavy breathing, heart racing. *I'm in trouble now. Place is surrounded. Me with my loaded M16—I already fired a round. Probably get charged with assault, assault with a deadly weapon. That's what sent Otis to the slammer, man: assault with a deadly weapon. I'm fucked. Shit hurts.*

"Come out with your hands up, Brown."

"Brown, I swear I never—"

Pain. Hurt. Injustice. He kept thinking: *Shit's so unfair. I'm in trouble now. Already fired a round. Facing a court-martial for sure. More busting in rank. Jail time. Behind bars in Leavenworth. End up as somebody's bitch getting ass-fucked up the Hershey Highway. Got buddies who did time, man, like Otis. He told me jail ain't no picnic. Jail is all divided by race, man—got to stick together 'cause it's a danger zone. Brothers stick together, crackers stick together, spics do the same 'cept if they're in rival gangs. Fights, rape, beatings. Slammer sucks big-time.*

"Come out with your hands up, Brown. This is your commanding officer."

Hurt. Injustice. Betrayal.

"PFC Brown, let Harrison go and come out with your hands up. I'll start counting from five. After the count, we will take measures to extract you."

Hurt. I'm hurting, man.

"Brown, this is your last warning. Let Harrison go and come out with your hands up so we can see them."

Injustice. Shit ain't right. Fuck, nothing makes sense.

"Five ... four ..."

Brown tilted his weapon up and pointed the muzzle to his head.

Harrison screamed, "Brown, don't ..."

"Three ... two ..."

Harrison leaped forward. Brown had his right thumb on the trigger and ...

"One."

MPs busted through both the front and back hooch doors. Their weapons were drawn.

CHAPTER 11

Brown here. I sure screwed up, y'all. Screwed the pooch. Game over. Fuck, the fat lady did sing. Nothing left. Nada. I'll soon be doing dirt time when I'm six feet under. That should be next week, right after the funeral. That's when they'll bury me—next week sometime. Right now my lifeless body is being flown back stateside, all because of my screwup.

Yeah, I killed myself yesterday, right there in our hooch at Camp America. That damn package, man. I wish I would've never gotten that damn package.

In case y'all are wondering how I can speak to you, the fact is ... I'm ... I'm a ghost. Yeah, that's right—I'm a ghost now. Shit's real, y'all. That ghost shit does happen. It happens often with violent deaths, like suicides and shit. Like my suicide.

There's two types of ghosts, y'all. One type is a ghost who don't know he's dead. That's a ghost who walks 'round everywhere and moves things around to get attention.

The second type of ghost is my type. We know we's dead, but our deaths were so violent and sudden, it's like a video we keep replaying. For me, I keep replaying what happened yesterday—being in hooch 1305 and blowing my brains out. That's where I am right now, back in hooch 1305, right where I blew my brains out yesterday.

Cool thing 'bout being a ghost is I can be anywhere I want to, and 'cause of that, I can see and hear shit anywhere and everywhere. That's why I know what really happened—at least most of what really happened. The rest I'm still searching for. I'm also monitoring the situation, putting the pieces together, listening to conversations and shit.

Bottom line, y'all, it was that twisted psycho bitch Tonya—Tywanna's jacked-up sister—who fucked everything up. I never liked Tonya; I knew she was always jealous of Tywanna and shit. I guess Tonya just wanted to cause trouble and see me and Tywanna break up. Shit, man, twisted Tonya sent me 'em photos. Sent the same ones to Harrison's wife. Now Harrison's probably facing the big D—a big fuckin' divorce—as soon as he makes it back home stateside. Lawyers, child custody battles, child support payments, alimony—all that shit's waiting for him.

Ya know, everything I see and hear says Harrison was right, man. Some sleeping pill or ecstasy ... some drug shit was involved. Tonya set the whole thing up at a club while Harrison was on leave and I was back at Gitmo. Tonya, or somebody she hired, photographed the whole thing: Harrison having sex with my Tywanna. I should've looked at them pics closer. Harrison and my T look completely out of it, completely drugged up, even if they're naked and shit and it looks like they're having sex. 'Course I wasn't thinking clear yesterday when I first saw that shit. I wasn't listening with both ears neither.

Then the e-mails, man. Psycho bitch Tonya somehow got hold of my e-mail address and made herself out to be Tywanna. Fuck, I wish I had been able to call Tywanna yesterday before I got that stupid package. Maybe things would've been different if I had talked to T over the phone. 'Course the waiting lines for the phones were huge. Who knows, man?

Shit sucks, y'all. And poor Tywanna—her drink was spiked just like Harrison's. I wish I had paid more attention to what Harrison was tellin' me yesterday—that he was drugged up and shit. Like I told y'all, I wasn't listenin' with both ears yesterday, not with me being all hot and steaming with my "King Kong ain't got nothing on me" attitude. Hell, I was thinkin' 'bout me being that owl looking for a moth. Power, man, power. That loaded M16 made me feel powerful.

'Course now there won't be no college, no more dreams of being a politician like Charles Rangel, no ETS, no marriage to T, no more time with Danielle. I won't see Jamaal's first child being born. I won't be an uncle, man. I'll also never be at Chantel's college graduation. All because I blew my brains out yesterday. All because of that twisted Tonya spiking drinks at a dance club.

Tells y'all what: Tonya is twisted all right, and she's clever too. Dance club—go there and find the best-looking dude, the sharpest dancer. She knows Tywanna likes to dance. Set things up, spike their drinks, drug 'em up. Once they's drugged up, you can undress them and photograph them and shit. Get the dude's wallet and get his address. What a bonus when the dude ends up being my squad leader. I'm still trying to figure out whether Tonya knew Harrison was my squad leader—I'm still monitoring that shit, man.

Fuckin' Tonya. See, Tonya's biggest problem—and she's got many problems—is she can't have kids. I know this now, now that I'm a ghost. Tonya herself knows 'cause the doctor told her she can't ever have kids. Shit's biological. Tonya's jealous that Tywanna has Danielle. Jealousy, man—that Tonya bitch is jealous.

That crap a couple years back 'bout Tonya having a miscarriage was all bullshit. I know 'cause I heard her confess yesterday when she was thinking 'bout it. She made the whole miscarriage thing up 'cause she wanted attention. She always wants attention.

And I'm dead … or am I? This ghost shit is like being caught up between life and death. I know I'm dead, but sometimes I still feel alive, man. Another dimension, I guess. I'm in some other dimension. I can still see and hear shit too.

The thing I was scared 'bout yesterday was the whole assault thing. I knew I was in deep shit … that it's wrong to fire a weapon. And the photos really hurt me too. Heck, facing a court-martial ain't no joke, y'all. All them stories my buddy Otis told me 'bout prison life didn't help me neither.

Fuck, man, knowing what I know now, I should've taken my chances with a court-martial. You know what they say: better to be judged by twelve than to be carried by six. Shit's real, y'all. I should've taken my chances with a court-martial, with a jury of twelve, instead of being carried away in a coffin by six pallbearers. That'll be me soon—funeral, pallbearers, six feet under doing dirt time. Game fucking over.

I know I'll let go of this "searching" stuff someday, and when that happens, then I won't be a ghost no more. But first I gotta keep searching and make sure all the missing pieces come together. There's one thing I do know: once I get that squared away, I'll be ready to cross over to the afterlife.

The missing piece? Shit, y'all, it's the fact that Tywanna's pregnant. Question is, who's the dad? I know it's either me or Harrison. See, Tywanna was faithful to me until twisted Tonya did her spiked-drink thing. Tywanna and me had sex during my R & R, but who knows, man, it could be Harrison too, even if the photos shows he's kinda outta of it. I want to know—who's the father of Tywanna's baby?

Man, I hope it's me. I hope I'm the dad. Heck, having a child is the only thing I got left in this fucked-up world, a world I ain't even a part of no more. I always treated Danielle as my own, but y'all know what I mean—leave something of yourself behind.

Right now, I'm in hooch 1305, thinkin' my shit over, playin' the same scene over and over in my head, thinkin' what I shoulda done different. Soon a squad from the Virginia National Guard will move into our hooch. The floor and the walls have already been painted to cover my bloodstains and shit.

Shit, y'all, as I'm checking up on things and searching to put all the pieces together, I'll leave with the words of advice Papa Smurf Rivera told me yesterday, two hours before our shift change: *shit happens, son, but the key is how you deal with it.*

That damn package, man. I wish I would've never gotten that damn package.

I'll Face Y'all!

JB

THE END

105

ABOUT THE AUTHOR

Paul Bouchard's books include *Enlistment, The Boy Who Wanted to be a Man,* and the nonfiction works *A Catholic Marries a Hindu* and *Lessons Learned.* For more on Paul Bouchard, visit www.authorpaulbouchard.com.